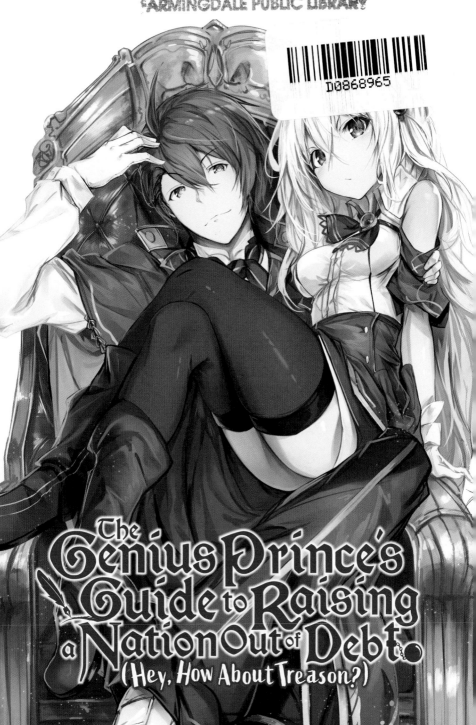

©Falmaro

Toru Toba Illustration Falmaro

The Genius Prince's Guide to Raising a Nation Out of Debt.
(Hey, How About Treason?)

©Falmaro

Imperial Ambassador
Fyshe Blundell

So it's true... He's the real deal.

©Falmaro

THIS COUNTRY
THE HELL OUTTA
EEEEERE!"

I know we're in the middle of a military campaign... but as a woman, I'm going to indulge in a bit of luxury, Wein.

©Falmaro

CONTENTS

The Genius Prince's Guide to Raising a Nation Out of Debt (Hey, How About Treason?)

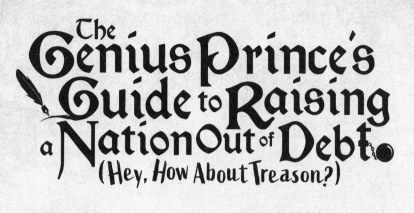

The Genius Prince's Guide to Raising a Nation Out of Debt
(Hey, How About Treason?)

1

Toru Toba

Illustration **Falmaro**

YEN ON

New York

The Genius Prince's Guide to Raising a Nation Out of Debt (Hey, How About Treason?)

Toru Toba

Translation by Jessica Lange
Cover art by Falmaro

This book is a work of fiction. Names, characters, places, and incidents are the product of the author's imagination or are used fictitiously. Any resemblance to actual events, locales, or persons, living or dead, is coincidental.

TENSAI OUJI NO AKAJI KOKKA SAISEI-JYUTSU ~ SOUDA, BAIKOKU SHIYOU ~ volume 1
Copyright © 2018 Toru Toba
Illustrations copyright © 2018 Falmaro
All rights reserved.
Original Japanese edition published in 2018 by SB Creative Corp.

This English edition is published by arrangement with SB Creative Corp., Tokyo in care of Tuttle-Mori Agency, Inc., Tokyo.

English translation © 2019 by Yen Press, LLC

Yen On
150 West 30th Street, 19th Floor
New York, NY 10001

Visit us at yenpress.com
facebook.com/yenpress
twitter.com/yenpress
yenpress.tumblr.com
instagram.com/yenpress

First Yen On Edition: August 2019

Yen On is an imprint of Yen Press, LLC.
The Yen On name and logo are trademarks of Yen Press, LLC.

The publisher is not responsible for websites (or their content) that are not owned by the publisher.

Library of Congress Cataloging-in-Publication Data
Names: Toba, Toru, author. | Falmaro, illustrator. | Lange, Jessica (Translator), translator.
Title: The genius prince's guide to raising a nation out of debt (hey, how about treason?) / Toru Toba ; illustration by Falmaro ; translation by Jessica Lange.
Other titles: Tensai ouji no akaji kokka saisei-jyutsu, souda, baikoku shiyou. English
Description: First Yen On edition. | New York, NY : Yen On, 2019-
Identifiers: LCCN 2019017156| ISBN 9781975385194 (v. 1 : pbk.)
Subjects: LCSH: Princes—Fiction.
Classification: LCC PL876.O25 T4613 2019 | DDC 895.6/36—dc23
LC record available at https://lccn.loc.gov/2019017156

ISBNs: 978-1-9753-8519-4 (paperback)
978-1-9753-8516-3 (ebook)

10 9 8 7 6 5 4 3 2 1

LSC-C

Printed in the United States of America

Two men strolled down the stone corridor of the royal palace in the Kingdom of Natra. They carried themselves with a certain dignity and pride—even their gait was refined. This was expected of these two longtime vassals of the kingdom.

One was a civil official. The other, a military officer. Though in separate spheres of influence, they were appointed around the same time and remained on friendly terms. In fact, they'd occasionally meet up at the palace to share a spirited discussion or two.

On this day, however, the hallway wasn't filled with their usual merry chatter, clouded instead by matching solemn looks.

There was only one reason for their gloom.

"His Royal Majesty's condition...doesn't look too promising," the civil official croaked in a voice thick with emotion.

Shutting his eyes tightly, the military officer sighed. "Well, with the weather wreaking havoc across the continent—it must be particularly rough on His Royal Majesty, given his physical condition..."

"Oh, the whims of the heavens! I've heard other countries are in shambles from losing key decision makers."

"You know, they say the Emperor himself has fallen ill. Thanks to that, the other royal courts have become dens of wily little devils."

The civil official sharply exhaled through his nose. "Sure, he might've managed to unite the Empire with his charisma, but they say the brighter the light, the darker the shadow becomes when it vanishes... I guess this is all the more true since they've yet to name a successor."

"Well, our own kingdom isn't much different. But unlike them, we have hope in…" He trailed off as a figure appeared on the far side of the corridor.

No sooner had they confirmed his identity than they immediately stepped aside to salute. This was a rare sight indeed. Not many people in the palace warranted such a display.

"Prince Wein. Good morning, Your Highness," they greeted in unison.

Standing before them was a young boy attended by a servant.

He was the crown prince of the Kingdom of Natra, Wein Salema Arbalest.

"Oh, morning," he replied.

He was only sixteen years old—a boy by most standards—but he'd just been appointed as the prince regent, tasked with running government affairs in place of the ailing king.

"What's with those cheerless expressions? …Is it about my father?"

The two reverently responded to Wein's inquiry.

"Yes, Your Highness," confirmed one.

"Our deepest apologies. When we received word about His Royal Majesty's condition…," started another.

"I see," Wein murmured quietly, placing his hands on their shoulders. "There's no need to worry any further. *I* am here."

They trembled lightly under his hands.

"Besides, it isn't just me. We have so many vassals supporting Father all these years. If we join hands, I'm certain we can overcome any national crisis."

"Your Highness…"

"That's for certain."

He serenely smiled over the pair fervently nodding. "There is no time to grieve. We cannot distract him from his recovery. I'll be expecting the two of you to step up and rise to the occasion."

""Y-yes, Your Highness!"" they crooned.

As he bid them farewell and continued down the corridor with his servant, the two gazed after him until he was out of sight, then they sighed and melted into a puddle of complete admiration.

"…Oh, I just knew it. Our shining beacon of hope."

"I couldn't agree more. I've heard he was gifted from an early age, but he's shown so much growth since returning from his studies in the Empire. He's already managed to stop chaos from erupting in the Imperial Court and is now working toward unifying the kingdom's vassals."

"Heh, I bet the Empire will have a jealous fit when they hear this."

"Let us throw more salt in the wound by further supporting His Highness's endeavors."

"Yes, of course."

The two nodded to each other—gone were their previously dark expressions. In their hearts, they were already imagining a bright future for their kingdom in the prince's hands.

At the very center of the royal palace was an office set aside for government affairs. Its heavy doors swung open to reveal Wein and his attendant as they stepped inside the room. It was strictly reserved for the king under normal circumstances. But things were far from that, and now Wein was using this room to conduct royal business.

He came to rest in front of a desk stacked with documents and papers. "Ninym, confirm my schedule for today."

His aide was an inconceivably beautiful girl around the same age as Wein, with near-transparent white hair and blazing-red eyes.

"In the morning, you are to check these reports and resolve any submitted disputes. In the afternoon, you are scheduled to attend a luncheon meeting and then three conferences, before paying His Royal Majesty a visit."

"That means no one will come in here all morning?"

"Correct."

Ah, very good. Wein nodded to himself, and then—he screamed at the top of his lungs.

"LET'S JUST SELL THIS COUNTRY OFF AND GET THE HELL OUTTA HEEEEEEEEEEERE! All that stuff about 'joining hands'? Yeah, total BS! This country's mess ain't so easy to fix! Not. A. Chance! We're. Totally. Screwed!"

"There you go again," Ninym chided, unfazed by this sudden outburst. She let go of her stiflingly formal tone. "Joking or not, you really shouldn't say those things out loud, Wein."

"It's no joke, Ninym! I'm totally serious!"

"That's even worse," she said with a sigh.

Here was the successor of the Kingdom of Natra, the boy expected to save them all—Wein Salema Arbalest.

In reality, he was actually a no-good slacker. In fact, his least favorite words were *duty, responsibility,* and *effort.*

"Ugh, you're always like this when you're out of the public eye… At least try being a little more professional, please," she lamented.

Ninym Ralei had been at his side since childhood, and as his chief aide, she was one of the few blessed with knowing his true personality. Some would say it went against common sense to assign a young girl as the aide of an equally adolescent crown prince turned regent. Doubly so because he was dealing with national politics.

However, no one in the kingdom's royal court would ever dare say that was the case—half out of fear of displeasing the crown prince who'd appointed her, half due to her personal achievements and displays of skill.

Wein was able to speak so openly with her because they'd established a relationship with each other, founded on mutual trust and cooperation. This also made them brutally honest when no one else was around. Nonetheless, there was a reason Wein was spitting out these absurd complaints, something that went beyond his own disposition.

"Hmm? C'mon, what's with the Little Miss Perfect attitude?! Ninym, you *do* realize this country's dirt-poor, right?!"

"'Dirt-poor' is an exaggeration… We simply have severe shortages of labor, resources, and capital. That's all."

"Yeah, that's what the rest of the world calls dirt-poor!"

To backtrack, the Kingdom of Natra was one of the many countries on the continent of Varno. With a population just under five hundred thousand, it was considered a relatively small country.

Located at the northernmost tip of the continent, the kingdom experienced short springs and long winters. Not only that, but the majority of the country's land was made up of barren rock and mountains.

Even though it boasted a long history, the country possessed limited resources and hardly any industry. In fact, the only thing it was really known for was its snowy landscapes, which brought in a handful of curious travelers every year. But to the average citizen, the bitter cold was more of a curse than a blessing.

Natra was a historic kingdom, but this was mostly due to its being such an unappealing target that other countries rarely looked its way, never mind actually invading. It's all thanks to wise and sensible rulers of the past that it's managed to maintain any semblance of a proper country up until now.

All in all, it was a small, vulnerable nation with more than enough potential to be swept away at any moment.

And that was putting it lightly.

"Our administration has no funds. And we don't have any industries to make any cash. We don't even have the military power to steal any from someone else. And anyone with half a brain ends up leaving the country in pursuit of better opportunities elsewhere! Now that Father's ill and that storm's brewin' across the continent, I'm stuck running the whole freakin' countryyyy!!"

Given all this, his complaining wasn't totally uncalled for. It was clearly a burden too heavy for a boy, especially one halfway through adolescence.

Not that there was anyone who could replace him.

"Agh, why'd I have to be born a prince of *this* country? If only I'd

been born in a place with more resources, manpower, and funds… You
know what? It's hopeless! We're totally gonna get invaded. Maybe we
can cut back on our resources… Oh, but if we involve too much manpower, we might incite a coup…"

"Oh, all right, enough with that doom and gloom. Here, get some
work done." Ninym pressed a fat stack of documents under his nose as
he continued to mutter his wild delusions.

"Agh," he moaned in a haunting tone, giving the papers a quick
glance before passing them back immediately. "Looks good. Next."

"…Did you read through them? *Properly?*"

"Yeah, yeah, I read 'em. Every last word. It said you gained weight,
and— Ow!! You—! I'm pretty sure it's considered improper to step on
the prince's foot!"

"Take your work more seriously if you want me to properly respect
you. Also, I haven't gained weight. Thank. You. Very. Much."

"Whaaat? Hey now, this won't do, Ninym! No, not at all. Did you
honestly think I wouldn't notice your footsteps getting heavier? I know
your body hardly ever changes, but I know for a *fact* you've gained
more than a pound since last week, and— Hey, quit it, stupid! Cut that
out! Don't twist my ar— GWAAAAAAA?!"

"Would you like to explore just how far your joints bend? Or will
you do your work?"

"I—I would very much like to work, please!"

"Very well, then. And for the record, I haven't gained any weight.
Am I clear?"

"Yes'm." He caved.

Ninym was the only one in the kingdom who could kick his butt
into shape.

"Agh! I can't take this anymore. All I want is to be left alone with
my mountain of gold coins, tease you, and live the easy life. Is that so
much to ask?"

Just as Wein stretched out across his desk to grumble further, a knock came from the office door. He bolted upright in a start as the door opened with a heavy clack.

It was a young girl.

"Are you in here, Wein?"

She certainly looked a bit younger than Ninym and Wein. As she flitted around the room, her summery dress and black hair danced around her. She embodied loveliness.

Certain parts of her face bore a striking resemblance to Wein's. Well, that much was to be expected. After all, she was Falanya Elk Arbalest, the younger sister of Wein Salema Arbalest…

In other words, the princess.

"—Oh, it's you, Falanya. What's up?" Making it seem as if he'd just finished a long bout of work, Wein casually straightened up and lifted his face out of the papers before him.

"Um, it's not anything important really. It's just… You've just been so busy lately, Wein. We've hardly had the chance to talk," confessed Falanya, looking up at him with hope in her glistening eyes. "…Am I bothering you?"

"As if." Wein smiled. "Any big brother who thinks that is a failure of a sibling. Come over here."

Her face lit up as she rushed over to Wein and hopped onto his knee.

"G-geez… Falanya, I know I said 'come over here,' but this is hardly proper."

"I don't see how that could be. This has been my spot since forever." She giggled, rubbing her cheek against his chest like an affectionate little pet.

Wein found his mouth relaxing into a goofy grin, but he reined it in whenever Falanya looked up at him. Meanwhile, Ninym scribbled something on a piece of paper for his eyes only: *Sister complex.*

Drop it, he scrawled.

Falanya tilted her head at him curiously. "Is there something wrong, Wein?"

"Oh, no, it's nothing. I was just thinking you're so light compared with a certain someone."

"Now, now. It's not very nice to compare people's weights."

"Ha-ha, you're right. I'm sorry," Wein said with a laugh, looking straight at Ninym.

I'm gonna kill you.

…Aaaaand he was just gonna pretend he didn't see that last one.

"I'm so relieved," Falanya said with a sigh. "I was afraid you'd be upset with me for getting in the way."

"……"

"Wein?"

"Oh, well, yeah, I've been at it nonstop. Right, Ninym?"

"Why, yes. Of course… In fact, just before Your Highness's arrival, Wein said he was displeased with the amount of work I'd given him. I think he insisted I give him more." Without missing a beat, Ninym whipped out a mountain of paperwork from an undisclosed location and dropped it on his desk. "I, Ninym Ralei, am in awe of Your Highness's tireless dedication to his duties as a regent."

"Oh my. Well, that's Wein for you."

"…Right?! It's only natural as a prince!" Wein chuckled with confidence while shooting Ninym the most damning glare.

She feigned ignorance.

"But you won't have much free time for a while, will you, Wein?"

"Yeah. The vassals have helped keep the royal court under control for the most part, but there are still problems in the kingdom. I'll be busy until we can find a solution… I'm sorry. The truth is, I'd really love to play with you."

"There's no reason to apologize," consoled Falanya, shaking her head. Her voice grew anxious. "But promise you won't push yourself too hard. If you collapsed like Father… Oh, I don't know what I'd do…"

"Don't worry. I may look scrawny, but I won't go down easy. And you're wrong if you think you can't help out."

"…What can I do?"

"It's not difficult: Just keep on smiling." He poked at her full cheeks. "As long as you keep that up, Falanya, Father and I will be just fine. This is your special power."

"Really?"

"Of course. I never lie to you… Mostly… Usually… Yeah, well, I'm telling the truth now."

"So…is this good?" She gave him a small smile, and he nodded sincerely with satisfaction.

"Wow, yeah, I'm feeling better already. But I think a hug would make it even better."

"Hee-hee-hee. Oh, you're so silly. Whee!" She giggled, jumping into his arms. "How's this?"

"Wow, that's perfect. I think I can power right through my work this afternoon. Today's a big day, so you're really helping me out."

"Oh, that makes me so happy… But what's so important about today?" Falanya tilted her face to look up at him as she continued to hold on to him tightly.

"I have a meeting with the Imperial ambassador."

©Falmaro

The Earthworld Empire was a large nation located on the eastern half of the Varno continent.

Blessed with a temperate climate and fertile lands, it was rich in mineral resources, and it boasted access to fisheries in one of the largest, most prized lakes on the continent. The Empire was abundant with essentially everything.

For that reason, it also had a long history of suffering foreign invasions, essentially since its founding. To fend them off, the Empire focused its efforts on military development, and before anyone had time to realize, it had become the strongest nation on the continent. When the current emperor rose to power, he consolidated those forces to occupy neighboring nations one by one. The continent was close to being unified under one leader for the first time in history.

At least, that was the case until the day the Emperor collapsed.

"—And that concludes my report on Crown Prince Wein Salema Arbalest."

"Thank you." In a room of the building provided for her, Fyshe Blundell emitted a small sigh as the aide wrapped up her report.

Fyshe looked to be in her midtwenties, and her winning feature was her flowing blond hair, which framed her stunning face. But woe to anyone who thought beauty was all there was to her. She was presently residing in the Kingdom of Natra as an Imperial ambassador of the Empire.

"Hmm, I suppose the rumors are true: He's wise and benevolent."

"Yes, he's been acknowledged domestically and internationally as the rightful heir to the throne. Even his recent appointment to regent went largely unopposed."

"I'm jealous, especially seeing how our own nation has been turned completely upside down. That aside, it's unfortunate we haven't been able to properly meet until today."

"Well, you relocated to Natra when you became the ambassador, right as he left to pursue his studies in the Empire."

Yes, Fyshe had first been assigned to the Kingdom of Natra several years prior. Through persistent negotiations, she'd built a decent relationship with the king over the years. But now, the situation had completely changed.

"I wonder how the crown prince will come at us today?"

"He'll likely get straight to the point... He can't afford not to. I've no doubt he'll bring up the Imperial troops stationed here."

At the moment, there were about five thousand troops stationed in Natra—a feat accomplished by a series of successful negotiations that secured official permission from their king. But Fyshe and her aide knew this foreign military presence was being met with anxiety and opposition by the people of the kingdom.

"Will he demand we withdraw?"

"I can't say for sure. It'll be important to pay attention to his position during the meeting. But let's also keep an eye out for his character... It should be easy to tell whether he's fit to be king. Well, all that being said, anyone who hires a Flahm is more than a little peculiar."

"You mean Ninym Ralei?"

"Who else? I mean, I knew many of them lived here, but I was surprised to see other countries besides the Empire appoint Flahm as vassals."

"My thoughts exactly. And it would seem this kingdom has a history of accepting them that is far older than ours. Natra must seem odd to nations in the West, since their people only treat the Flahm as slaves."

"When the Empire finally unifies the continent, we'll eradicate such senseless values and traditions... Well then, let us head to the meeting." Fyshe stood from her chair.

This was the first time they'd be coming together for official business and exchange words beyond a few simple pleasantries.

"If our information is correct, our lack of progress is nearing its end.

We *must* ensure our troops remain here, no matter what." With a firm resolve, she set out for the meeting.

"Fyshe Blundell was originally an ambassador to Vanhelio," Ninym commented, feeding Wein some basic information as she trailed after him down the corridor of the royal palace

"Say, Vanhelio is a large nation in the West. Why would she come here?"

When they were in public, their speech was strictly that of master and servant. Not that speaking this way was particularly difficult. They had a long time to practice and adjust to switching back and forth.

"Well, she was caught up in political turmoil occurring in her homeland and ended up in Natra while you were in the Empire. She may not be rising through the ranks anymore, but she's still very skilled and talented."

"If she's that good, then I bet she's bored of living in our rural kingdom."

"Actually, according to her, she is quite satisfied. Our sources have said she's openly stated she's weary of dealing with politics."

He smiled wryly. "I see. Whatever the case may be, I'm delighted to hear outsiders taking a liking to our nation. But if she's that brilliant, I don't anticipate this meeting to be a straightforward one."

"The issue at hand is the occupying Imperial soldiers...," Ninym mentioned. "This will be tricky."

Wein sighed inwardly. *Yeah, can't argue with that.*

To begin with, why were they even in Natra? On paper, they were using the region to practice drills. That wasn't the whole truth, of course.

There were a number of factors at play, but they all led to the same core issue: The Kingdom of Natra was in a vulnerable geographic location.

Imagine a rough ellipsis. Let's say that's the continent of Varno.

Next, picture the Giant's Backbone, a mountain range stretching from north to south, dividing the continent into two equal halves. It acted as a barrier between East and West, resulting in completely different policies, races, ideologies, and cultures between the two.

Of course, it wasn't as if travel between them was impossible. In fact, plenty of roads connecting the two halves had been established in recent years. Unfortunately, most of these paths were only useful for trade and private travel.

Compare those roads to the blood vessels in the human body. To take this analogy further: An artery would be a major road that could support the comings and goings of hundreds of thousands of soldiers. There are relatively few major arteries in a human body, and they serve an incredibly vital function—similarly, these roads hold immense commercial and militaristic value.

For a country aiming for complete dominion, one might even say these roads would be indispensable.

And it was directly through the Kingdom of Natra that the continent's northernmost artery ran. In its bid to control the Western lands, this was not a place the Empire could ignore.

Why did this happen?

When the Empire stationed its soldiers here, it paid a considerable sum of money for the privilege. It wasn't a one-sided agreement.

That said, having foreign soldiers on the kingdom's land was like having a knife pressed to the throat. It made the citizens nervous, and the domestic troops didn't approve, either.

Well, to be exact, the military was expecting Wein to force the Imperial soldiers to withdraw.

It wasn't as if he didn't share their sentiments. After all, it wasn't *just* a concern for national security: It was a matter of honor. But there was a reason Wein was unable to grant their wish.

And that reason was… Drumroll, please.

Frankly, I wanna butter 'em up!

And there it was.

Honestly, going up against a huge country would be a huge pain in the ass, and we could really use the money. I'm totally fine with the whole deal, really...

First and foremost, Wein had studied in the Empire, meaning he had a solid understanding of their military prowess.

But ignoring the wishes of his troops would also present a problem.

I mean, the only reason my rise to regent was so smooth in the first place was because the vassals have high hopes for me. If I disappoint them by immediately wagging my tail at the Empire, it'll make things tough from here on out. And if I tick off the military, there's the possibility of a coup.

He was damned if he did and damned if he didn't. As Wein internally lamented and moaned over his crisis, he realized his aide was gone.

"Ninym?"

"—Pardon me." Ninym appeared from the shadows. "We've just received word from our spies in the Empire."

"Word...?"

She handed him a letter. Wein read its contents.

"...Hmm, is that so?" He cocked an eyebrow. "There's no doubt that the ambassador caught wind of this, too... In that case..." He closed his eyes for a moment, then started forward. "Let's go, Ninym. I've got a plan."

"R-right... But what's your plan, again?"

"I've decided," Wein hinted with a grin. "We're takin' it all."

"It's been quite some time, Your Highness," greeted Fyshe Blundell upon Wein's arrival, Ninym in tow. With her aide by her side, she'd been waiting for them in the reception room. "I have made your acquaintance on a previous occasion, but allow me to formally introduce myself again: I am the ambassador of the Earthworld Empire, Fyshe Blundell."

"And I am the prince of the Kingdom of Natra, Wein Salema Arbalest."

With that, they sat down.

Fyshe was the one to start off the talks.

"Thank you for meeting with me. Please accept my sincerest con-gratulations on Your Highness's ascension to prince regent. I do hope I am not too bold in saying we keenly feel the kingdom's grief over His Royal Majesty the King's condition and see your promotion as the only silver lining among these darkest of times."

"Thank you, Ambassador Blundell. I know I'm carrying the hopes and dreams of many on my shoulders. I intend to do my best not to betray my people. I look forward to working together to foster a cordial relationship between Natra and Earthworld."

"Of course, Your Highness."

The meeting began on a harmonious note.

The two exchanged pleasantries and discussed topics with no real meaning or consequence. Or it might appear that way. In reality, they were sizing each other up and taking note of their opponent's char-acter. On one hand, you had an acting head of state. On the other, the ambassador of a powerful nation. They sat face-to-face, eyeing each other. You might even call it a joint effort.

The tension in the room bubbled, palpable in the air. The audience observing them understood: This initial conversation was a calculated, critical dance to find out who had more of an edge.

So it's true... He's the real deal... Fyshe reminded herself not to underestimate him. *Usually, the young and inexperienced want to see immediate results... But he acts like he has all the time in the world. He doesn't let his title get to his head but also speaks easily with someone of my station. He just became regent, but he has a regal air.*

But she knew her questioning would be thorough, and her talking points were solid. Having said that, she would not resort to under-handed tactics or aggressive interrogations. She needed to remain calm. This opponent was very hard to read.

When she was his age, she certainly didn't have this much wisdom and tact. She knew this much for sure.

If I'm not careful, I'm done for... She set her senses to high alert and braced herself.

As Fyshe was busy with her own thoughts, something else distracted Wein from the task at hand.

Holy. Her boobs are huge...

He was the worst of the worst.

I didn't notice when she introduced herself, but wow. They're really somethin' else... I know they're two bundles of fat, but it's like they've taken on a life of their own. Is it because the Empire's overabundant in pretty much everything? I mean, when you compare 'em... Wein turned around to look at Ninym, who was jotting down notes behind him. Well, more specifically, at her breasts.

...Yep. The gap in destructive power is pretty obvious.

Whir! Her quill pen stabbed the back of his head.

"Ow...!"

"Your Highness?"

"Ah, no, just a bit of a headache. I guess losing sleep over work isn't the best idea," he suggested, in a hurry to smooth things over.

Ninym passed a document to him from behind. *Be serious,* it said.

How the hell did she know what I was thinking? He shivered at the thought of women's intuition.

He was still considering this frightening idea when Fyshe smiled gently at him.

"—At any rate, I feel as though a weight's been lifted. To tell the truth, I had some concerns prior to our meeting about forming good relations with Your Highness. But this has assured me those fears were unfounded."

"I'm glad hear you say so, Ambassador. This partnership will certainly help me out and solve some of my worries."

"Well, I assume you have a never-ending list of worries, now that you're taking over the duties of your office?"

"Like trying to drink the sea. Pleasing your citizens, meeting with foreign nations, forming relations with the nobility, strengthening the military, increasing funds, supporting our industries... I take many things into consideration."

"Which would also include," she said, her eyes glinting shrewdly, "our soldiers stationed here."

The air froze.

The prelude had come to an end. The true battle was about to begin.

Well, how are you going to respond? Fyshe eyed him carefully.

Wein opened his mouth. "Maintaining relations with the Empire is my top priority."

"In that case—," she started.

"However," he interrupted, "the truth is, the presence of a foreign military makes my own troops uneasy."

But his confession had no effect on Fyshe. She'd expected he might say that: He wanted to save face with the Empire and still win over his people. Now it was time for her to negotiate—with funds or commodities—until they conceded. She had predicted those concessions were his aim, of course, and had come fully prepared.

This was exactly why Wein's next statement bewildered her.

"So I plan on removing the source of their worries."

"Wha...? 'Removing,' you say?"

"Yes. As I mentioned before, I'm very interested in maintaining a cordial relationship with the Empire. To do that, we should attempt to bridge the gap between the two, don't you think?"

"...You're right."

This is bad.

It was clear he had some sort of ulterior motive, but she couldn't figure it out in time. He was setting the pace of their conversation instead of following her lead. But she couldn't regain the initiative at this very moment, not now. It wasn't the time to set things straight.

"I'd like to take this opportunity to restructure the kingdom's military."

"Restructure your military...?"

"It pains me to admit our armed forces are weak. After all, we haven't spent much time on a real battlefield. This inexperience and naïveté has caused friction with the Empire and prevented us from forming a real partnership."

"And you want to smooth things over by overhauling your military organization?"

"Exactly. The problem is we won't see any progress or growth if we continue to rely only on our limited knowledge, and we don't have the necessary funds to carry it out to boot." Wein smirked. "So, Ambassador Blundell. Could the Empire give us their funds and military expertise?"

Fyshe stood dumbfounded.

But it wasn't just her. Her aide and Ninym were also seized by shock and agitation.

How stupid! There's no way we'd accept those terms! her aide screamed internally.

A crease formed between Ninym's brow. *Requesting the Empire to not only train our kingdom's military but also pay for it… That's way too unreasonable! Maybe he's starting big so his next request seems more fair?*

The two instinctively shot Wein a skeptical look.

But it was no use.

He was convinced his plan was perfectly sane. And in truth, Fyshe's reaction was vastly different from the two aides as she sat across from him.

"…Will this resolve our strife?"

"This small gesture will be enough to reach the hearts of my men. And I plan on doing my part to solve the problem as well."

"……"

She sank into silence, though her mind was a maelstrom. With all eyes on her, she finally caught up with her thoughts enough to speak again. "Understood. We can discuss the conditions at a later date, but…we will accept this proposal."

"Thank you, Ambassador. I thought you might understand."

They shook hands firmly as their aides stared and stared in disbelief.

"WHEW. I. AM. BEAT!"

With the burning sun dipping below the horizon, the moon started to shine in the night sky. His duties done for the day, Wein made a beeline for his room and dived onto his bed.

"Aghhh, enough already. I can't take this anymore. Why is being regent so exhausting? We went hard today, so let's take tomorrow off. And the day after that and the day after that."

"You know we can't." Ninym sighed, watching him roll around on the bed. "That aside, Wein, there's something I'd like to ask."

"My sincerest apologies, but we're closed for the day. I'm going to sleep now, so I ask all Ninyms to please return to their quarters for the evening."

"It'll only take a second."

"…You're not gonna let this go, huh?"

"No."

He huffed. "Fine. As long as you add *meow* to the end of every sentence from now until bedtime."

"……"

"Hey, hey, c'mon! What's wrong, Niny*meow*?! Does your embarrassment outweigh your curiosity?!"

"…Fine, *meow*."

"Hmm?! I can't hear you, *meow*! It'll be a problem if you don't speak up, MWROOOOW, MY ARM DOESN'T BEND THAT WAY!"

"Don't get cocky, *meow*."

"I-I'm sorry, *meow*…," he whimpered. "Well, lemme guess: You're going to ask me why Boobies went along with my plan, right?"

"'Boobies,' huh…? Anyway! You're not wrong."

"*Meow.*"

"…Anyway, you're not wrong, *meow*."

Ignoring Ninym's look of protest, he continued on in high spirits.

"Do you remember the news about the Empire, the message we got right before the meeting?"

"Hmm? Yes, of course... The Emperor of Earthworld seems to be recovering, right?"

"That's the reason."

"What do you mean? ...*Meow.*"

He rose from his bed.

"Listen. Our kingdom holds the key to one of the roads that link East and West, but compared to the other paths, it's totally run-down and basically unusable. That's exactly why the Empire dispatched their soldiers here—to prevent other countries from conquering us as they try to gain access to better roads. When the time comes, we're going to become a vassal state to the Empire through either military force or diplomacy... Or at least that's what was supposed to happen."

"But their plan fell through when the Emperor become ill."

"Right. The Imperial Court's a mess: They're losing control over their conquered territories and putting out the embers of an inevitable internal rebellion on their own. To buy themselves time, they have to play nice with small, weak countries like us."

"But he's recovered now... I don't understand. They have no obligation to help restructure our army, especially now. I mean, they'd be intentionally strengthening a potential enemy. Or maybe they're planning to crush us the moment after we manage to grow only slightly stronger...*meow.*"

Wein nodded. "They know that even if we attack them, they'll be able to handle us with force. But that's not really what they're after. To the Empire, we're nothing but a foothold: Their real endgame is conquering the West. Think about it. What does a country need to gain control of a continent?"

"'What,' you ask? Well, funds, food, equipment, and..." She trailed off and gasped. Her eyes flew wide-open, and she looked at him incredulously.

He flashed a quick grin. "You got it. Fyshe Blundell's aim is..."

◆◇◆

"Train Natra soldiers to serve in our Imperial troops...?!"

"That's right."

Meanwhile, Fyshe was nodding and exchanging words with her aide in another room.

"You've heard the good news of His Imperial Majesty the Emperor's recovery, right? I'm sure we'll advance into the West again. When the time comes, we'll be glad to have more soldiers."

"......"

"At first glance, this exchange seems to place the burden solely on the Empire. But since the kingdom is practically destined to become part of the Empire, think of the military instruction and financial contribution as an early investment. We have nothing to lose and everything to gain."

"Please wait," the aide objected. "I must ask something before we move forward. What assurance do we have that they won't bare their fangs at us?"

It was a perfectly reasonable question, but Fyshe'd already prepared an answer. "He won't strike at the Empire. His proposal is proof of that. Say their soldiers grew to rival the Empire's. Do you really believe we'd lose?"

"Of course not. It would be...impossible. We're much too strong."

"Precisely. He seems to understand this. You might ask: What's the meaning behind his proposal? To ingratiate himself to his army? No, nothing that superficial. It was a calculated move to protect his people."

"What do you mean?"

"He was probably aware of the Emperor's recovery, meaning he foresaw our strategy to continue our march into the West. What would happen to Natra then? They have only two options: fight or surrender diplomatically. Either choice would be their final act as a sovereign nation. In that case, which one would be better?"

The aide's eyes widened. "He proposed this to avoid falling under our complete control...?!"

"Yes. I mean, Natra's a pitifully small country that the Empire could easily polish off. If some high official in the Empire was after military exploits, an invasion of the kingdom is entirely possible. But this is a totally different story if their soldiers are positioned to join our army."

"So he's moving toward a diplomatic solution to form an allegiance... This will avoid needlessly spilling the blood of his citizens. And things will go smoothly for the both of us if we don't resort to military force—fewer lingering grudges and less aggression."

"In other words, he's appealing to his people and the provisional government by positioning this arrangement as an advantage. At the same time, he's laying the groundwork for a smooth transition, knowing they're destined to join the Empire... I must say, I'm impressed."

In spite of herself, Fyshe admired his strategy, his quiet stoicism during the meeting, and the ingenuity of his grand plan. The fact that this was coming from a sixteen-year-old kid made it all the more frightening.

She didn't know how he'd respond when Natra was annexed—but if he stepped down from power, she'd welcome him to the Empire with open arms.

Well, she did have one concern.

...Is this his only goal?

She accepted this plan when she saw an advantage. But he must have seen this coming, seeing that everything was going according to his plan.

Was it some sort of setup?

I left nothing to chance. I crushed every gap and loophole. It'd be impossible to fall into a trap... I'm sure of it.

But there was still a lingering sense of what-if.

Wein Salema Arbalest might possess more knowledge than she'd imagined.

I hate to admit it... But I can't deny he's very competent.

She couldn't rule out any possibilities, so she knew she needed to keep a sharp eye out for him and kept the image of Wein lingering in the back of her mind.

◆◇◆

"—Well, it's not a trap!"

"What are you going on about all of a sudden?"

"I just figured they're probably jumping at shadows right now."

Ninym flashed a dubious look at Wein, and he placated her, signaling *Don't worry about it* with his eyes.

"Anyway, you know why they went along with my conditions, right?"

"…Yeah."

"But your expression's telling me otherwise."

"I don't agree with your reasoning," Ninym emphasized in dissatisfaction. "Even if you're successful in receiving aid from the Empire, you've just sealed our fate! We're heading toward our demise." She hesitated. "…Do you really plan on surrendering?"

"Sure, that's the plan… Hey, hold it—don't twist my arm."

Ninym had wordlessly clawed into him.

"You should know! You were with me during my time in the Empire. They're ridiculously strong: Defying them would only result in bloodshed. Besides, I watched how they operate. They weren't so bad, y'know? Sure, it'll raise some concerns when we become their territory. But we'll adapt soon enough."

"…And how do you truly feel?"

"With this, I can say good-bye to this annoying-ass job and YEO-OOOOW MY ARM, MY ARM, MY ARM?!"

"I'm sure you can do it, Wein. You can stand against the Empire."

"Nah, sounds like a pain… UWAAAAAH, MY ARM SHOULDN'T BEND THAT WAY!"

She made him writhe and scream for a little while longer before dropping his arm and accepting defeat, turning her back toward him.

"If you hate it so much, betray me," he whispered soothingly. "Kill me, and this will go up in smoke. Hey, Ninym, my heart, you listening to this?"

"…You know your heart wouldn't do that to you."

No matter how much she cried out or protested or disagreed with his decisions, she would never defy them in the end. Her ancestors had taken a vow of absolute loyalty when they first came to this country and began to serve the royal family.

"Oh, don't sulk now. I get that you're feeling reluctant, but all countries disappear sooner or later. We just happen to be next in line."

"…Will our troops really accept this?"

"I'm sure they'll be upset at first. But we'll convince them we're biding our time to plan a counterattack or something. Once they see the Empire's strength for themselves, I'm sure their urge to revolt will subside. And when the time finally comes, they'll be ready to pledge allegiance to the Empire, and all our government positions will be reassigned, allowing me to take my money and live the good life! It's the perfect plan, if I do say so myself!"

"…I hope it fails."

He chuckled in high spirits. "Don't you know schemes are my forte? Just you wait. Also, you're forgetting something, Ninym."

"…Meow."

"Good girl."

She sighed even deeper in the face of her master's hubris.

Despite Ninym's wishes, Wein's predictions were coming true one after the other. Yes, there was some opposition among the soldiers to receiving instruction from the Imperial troops, but the military began carrying out his plans after he insisted they follow his lead.

The results were dramatic. Utilizing the doctrine and wealth of the most powerful nation on the continent, the Kingdom of Natra's armed forces rapidly grew in strength.

At the three-month mark, their troops were more powerful than they'd ever been.

"Yep, things are goin' my way! Wow, it's hard being right all the freakin' time!"

The new and improved Wein was in a fine mood. His office had once been a hub for angry grumbling, complaining, and wallowing in self-pity, but it'd since transformed into a place where he could be heard humming a peppy tune on any given day.

"Your efforts to bolster our strength appear to be going well," admitted Ninym, who was next to him. She still didn't look entirely convinced, but she acknowledged the results nonetheless. "But someone will get the better of you if you're arrogant and careless."

"Oh, come on, Ninym. Who could possibly pull the rug out from under me *now*? Barring some major natural disaster crippling the *entire* continent, the rest's all procedural stuff. I'm ready to think about what I'll do with my retirement."

"Seriously..." She gazed at him in weary discontent as he prattled on and on about traveling around the continent.

But he was interrupted by a sharp knock from the office window. Perched on the ledge, a bird with a cylindrical object attached to its leg was repeatedly bashing the pane with its beak.

It was one of Ninym's messenger birds.

She opened the window to untie the missive from its leg. "We have urgent news from our spies in the Empire."

"Urgent news? What, has the emperor suddenly decided to deploy his troops or something?"

"Let me see..." As she consulted the contents of the letter, the blood was sapped out of her face. "......The Emperor has died."

"Wha?" Wein blinked.

The office was strangely silent.

They locked eyes, but every other part of their body was frozen in place. They must have looked like a pair of lambs tossed onto a deserted field.

"...S-s-s-somehow I feel like I heard something heinous, but no, it's probably—*no*, most likely...*no*, most DEFINITELY a mistake, so read it again, Ninym, just to be safe... What did it say?" he sputtered.

"The Emperor of Earthworld has died."

"......" Wein buried his face in his hands and looked up at the ceiling. "I see... So the Emperor died——," he finally vocalized, testing it out on his tongue.

"WHAAAAAAAAAAAA?! He died?! Died?! The guy freakin' up and *DIED*?! But wait, I thought they said he recovered or whatever! Hey, what the *hell* is goin' on here?!"

"His condition had taken a turn for the worse, so he was resting as much as he could. But this appears to be rather...sudden."

"C-could it be some kind of mistake?!"

"They've already made an official announcement within the Empire... They could have kept it under wraps, but I imagine there were some political dealings going on within the Imperial Court."

"NOOOOOOOO!" he yelped, frantically tearing at his hair. "Th-this is bad. This is very bad. Wait, hold on. What about our deal? Let's see, uh, if the Emperor dies, that means Natra is...is..."

He was interrupted once again by a violent knock on the door, which flew open as a panicked messenger stumbled in.

"Pardon me, Prince Wein! It seems the Empire's troops have begun to move out!"

Whaaaaaaaaat?! By some strange miracle or perverse luck, he managed to stop his screams from blasting out of his mouth.

Not that the messenger took any notice of Wein's inner turmoil. He hurriedly continued with his report. "We believe they're heading toward the eastern border! Their destination is unknown! Commander Raklum wishes to know if he should pursue!"

Wein's thoughts raced around and around as he listened: The Emperor's untimely death. Imperial troops approaching the border. The two were clearly connected.

Then the next person up is——

His premonition soon came true.

"Please wait! I will mediate this!"

"Imperial Ambassador, please stay back!"

"I beg of you! There's no time!"

There was a scuffle on the other side of the open door. He could hear

©Falmaro

a group of people arguing back and forth as one voice grew more and more shrill and insistent. Ninym subtly attempted to stand between Wein and the door, blocking the way with her hands.

He could already guess who was about to appear in front of them.

"Your Highness!"

Of course, Fyshe Blundell was the one stomping around and pushing past the guards.

She immediately knelt before Wein. "I understand it is impudent of me to cause such a commotion in your palace! However, I must speak with you immediately!"

"...I hear your soldiers are moving toward the border," muttered Wein, shooting an icy glance in her direction. "The Empire has every right to do so. But why wasn't this discussed earlier? Was I wrong to assume we were committed to forging good relations?"

...But it's not like I can say aaaaaaaanything else!

You would never guess from his composure that Wein was writhing in agony inside.

I get it! I'm panicking, too! But she can't just come bursting in here! Oh, come on! It'll be impossible to talk in secret with everyone else in the room! If we were alone, I could have gone along with her plan or something!

The messenger, the guards, Ninym—their eyes bored into Wein and Fyshe as everyone waited with bated breath.

"Please accept my sincerest apologies...! I promise we have no ill intentions!"

"Well, why else would they be on the move?"

"...We received an order from the homeland. Our troops are to report back as quickly as possible."

"And what might be the reason for this order?"

"......" Fyshe hesitated, worried about discussing sensitive information here.

But she needed to reveal this information to convince others around her.

She admitted: "It's because His Imperial Majesty the Emperor...has crossed the great divide..."

This confession rippled through the room, echoing and ricocheting again and again.

…How could this happen? With her head bowed low, her heart was heavy with great torment and affliction.

The reason for this reaction was…*not* the Emperor's death. It wasn't even the reckless actions of their troops. No, it was her regret for failing to see through Wein's plan.

The Emperor had many loyal followers and servants, and while Fyshe had her own agenda, she counted herself among them. This devotion was why this entire situation was so unexpected. In fact, to be completely honest, she'd actively avoided thinking about the possibility: What would become of them if the Emperor passed away right while they were helping make Natra's troops stronger?

But he *didn't revere our emperor the same way. He'd planned for this to happen the entire time…!*

With the exception of forcible military occupation, it was normal for stationed troops to withdraw and report back to their homeland in the face of domestic strife. This was doubly true if they were on friendly terms with the nation in question.

As part of the Department of Foreign Affairs, Fyshe couldn't stop it from happening. It wouldn't do much good. Aside from appealing to the troops directly, she was in no position to give orders and lacked the authority to stop them from returning home.

But this left behind a whole army of soldiers in Natra, fully trained and funded by the Empire. They couldn't possibly be integrated into the Imperial army until things settled down.

I was so preoccupied by our advance to the West, but he was considering each and every scenario.

She couldn't deny Wein's intuition and skill. She had lost. As frustration and admiration mixed and swirled together in her heart, Fyshe began to ponder. *What was he thinking? What kind of brilliance flickered behind those cold eyes?*

She'd never guess the answer: *Oh, hell no! They tooooooootally think I pulled a fast one over the Empire!!*

But she was better off not knowing what was flailing inside of him.

"We have no intention of invading the Kingdom of Natra. Our goal is to swiftly return to our homeland. Please allow our troops to withdraw. It is out of respect for the Emperor," she begged, bowing her head.

If this prince was foolish, he'd use this as an opportunity to shoot their troops from behind.

"…Understood. Please accept my deepest condolences for your loss and relay this message to your loyal officers and soldiers. If they must immediately report home to the Empire, we will not interfere."

"You have my gratitude."

"It's a shame we'll have to end this training halfway through, but I assume there are important matters that must be dealt with. I hope peace will settle onto your lands as soon as possible."

"…Thank you."

As news of the Emperor's passing traversed the continent, it left behind a great sense of unease among the various nations—alongside ambition and a desire to use this to their advantage.

It has been said that on this day, a mournful wailing echoed through the royal palace, but no detailed records of this incident remain. "WHY MEEEEEEE?!"

The Earthworld Empire had been enjoying a golden age since its founding, spearheaded by a charismatic emperor and supported by his loyal officials and soldiers. The entire continent of Varno was well aware of their splendor. The people of the Empire were proud that they were a part of this glorious age and took it for granted that each successive day would shine brighter than the last.

But this vision came crashing down all too easily.

Following the Emperor's death, Earthworld dissolved into complete and total mayhem, and the stormy clouds of uncertainty settled over their future. They depended on the civil officials to keep the Empire from stumbling in the crisis—but the Imperial Court transformed into a den of thieves overnight as all scrounged for more power. Losing their guiding sun, the officials revealed their true nature, unleashing their dark hunger for more power.

Of course, there were those who wished to put a stop to this.

Fyshe Blundell, who had returned home from the Kingdom of Natra, was one of them.

...Sadly, I'm much too spineless.

Exiting a room in the Imperial Court, she let out a stifled sigh.

Her aide rushed over to greet her from her post outside. "How did it go, Ambassador?"

"They've placed me under house arrest for the time being."

The recent incident with the Kingdom of Natra was her own doing. This was the day they'd dole out her punishment.

"Thank goodness. They were more lenient than expected. I'm sure your track record was a deciding factor."

"It's safe to say it's because they don't want me meddling with their affairs anymore."

The Kingdom of Natra may have pulled one over on her, but it was a minor country all the same. There were countless more important things to be done here in the Empire. Indeed, an untold number of things. Fyshe had plenty to do, of course.

But she somehow couldn't let it go.

"Just when the Empire needs me most, and yet…"

It was incredibly frustrating. *Ugh!* Her heart filled to the brim with self-hatred.

"You mustn't, Ambassador. If you do something while under house arrest, they'll mete out a harsher punishment."

"I'm well aware of that. I intend to behave myself," she pledged. "But conducting research should be fine, right?"

"Research on…what, exactly?"

"The crown prince of Natra."

Her aide looked concerned. "Ambassador, I understand that you were bested, but you *must* move on," she urged.

"I don't care about that. I'm neither angry nor upset with him."

She was being honest. Sure, she'd have more peace of mind if she blamed everything on him, but she still held him in high regard. He'd held nothing back, and she accepted her defeat.

The past was in the past. Next time, she'd get him for sure.

"Based on intuition alone, he's likely to have made rapid progress. It may be only a matter of time before he bares his claws at the Empire. I simply wish to prepare our country to ensure we nip it in the bud."

"You may be overthinking matters… But if you insist, Ambassador, I will gladly assist."

Fyshe smiled. "I appreciate your help. First, let's research the time he spent studying in the Empire. I already know a decent amount, but we may uncover something new."

"Understood. Well then, I'll arrange for a thorough inspection of the archives," the aide confirmed before running off to carry out Fyshe's orders.

Fyshe peered out the window to look at the sky, connecting her to the West and the Kingdom of Natra.

"…I wonder what that little prince is doing right about now." She chuckled as she strolled down the hallway with thoughts of a worthy adversary weighing on her mind.

It'd been two months since the Imperial army left the Kingdom of Natra.

Wein gazed down upon hundreds of his soldiers neatly lined up before him, operating as one living, breathing unit, precisely obeying the orders of their commanding officer. Each move was spirited. The mere sight of it was breathtaking.

"What do you think, Your Highness?"

"Excellent work," he praised, nodding to his vassal in satisfaction as he watched the scene from his hilltop pavilion. "I was worried we might wander off course after losing Imperial guidance, but you've done a great job polishing them up so far. I was right to entrust them to you, Raklum."

"Thank you!" belted out Raklum, respectfully bowing his head.

Though the man was tall with a solid build, he wasn't the least bit intimidating. This was thanks to his unremarkable facial features, though one could perhaps consider his longer-than-average arms unique. He was one of the commanding officers of the Natra army and handpicked by Wein himself.

"Be that as it may, Your Highness, all I did was follow orders. I am not deserving of such high praise."

"I know how hard it is to find vassals fit for this job," Wein insisted. "The fact that it was done at all is thanks to you."

"But Your Highness was the one who selected and assigned me to this esteemed post. My deeds are hardly worth a grain of sand," Raklum said, pushing back.

"...Honestly, you never change," Wein said with a sigh, causing his officer to bow his head even more deeply.

Then a charming giggle interrupted their exchange. "Tee-hee, you two are so funny!"

It was Wein's younger sister, Falanya.

"Sorry, Falanya. Are you bored?"

"Not at all. It's interesting to watch the soldiers move with such grace, and I enjoy listening to your conversations. But, Raklum, you really ought to receive his praise. I'm a bit jealous, to be honest. He hardly ever praises me."

"You heard her, Raklum." Wein looked over at him with a wry smile.

With a complicated expression, Raklum finally spoke up. "...I will carve Your Highness's words into my heart."

"Seems you can't stand up against my little sister, either. Good work, Falanya. You deserve some praise for that."

"Oh no. If you praise me for this, I'm afraid I'll have to make Raklum act even more stubborn from now on," she teased.

The siblings burst into laughter together. Even Raklum let out a small smile.

"By the way, Wein, I haven't seen Ninym around recently. Is everything well?"

"Hmm? Ah, I had some business I could trust only Ninym with."

After all, she'd been chosen at birth to serve Wein and had undergone special training for this role, making her incredibly capable of handling any job flawlessly.

"How rare. It may be for work, but I'm surprised you allowed her to leave your side," Falanya admitted.

That was the truth. On the whole, Ninym never left Wein's side.

"It couldn't be helped. I couldn't trust this with anyone else."

He'd been reluctant, of course. With her help, it felt as though he could soar over a mountain instead of walk it. When he thought about his mounting piles of work for the day, he couldn't help but groan a little in his mind.

Well, he *could* theoretically get someone else to take care of it—but it'd actually be pretty difficult. After all, Wein was the only one who could substitute for the king. With his father appointing the majority of the vassals, their allegiance lay with the king and nation—not Wein. So far, Ninym and Raklum were the only ones who'd pledged their loyalty solely to him and possessed enough talent to participate in high-level politics. Aside from assigning Raklum to carry out the drills, he had no one else to take care of important matters, other than Ninym.

"Could this work concern the Empire by any chance?" Falanya asked.

"Hmm? What makes you think that?"

"I hear you've been buying lots of weapons from the Empire lately."

Hmm, noted Wein. Well, it wasn't as though he'd been trying to hide anything.

But Falanya had apparently caught wind of it. Perhaps this crisis had finally sparked an interest in politics and a desire to help him out.

"I'm buying weapons—yes. But my mission for Ninym is a separate matter. Well, okay, it's not *totally* separate, but…," continued Wein as he petted his sister's head.

An idea zapped into his mind.

"Say, Falanya, do you know *why* I'm buying weapons from the Empire?"

It wouldn't hurt to make this a teaching moment. She'd shown interest in the matter, after all.

She apparently understood why he was asking her this, as she thought carefully before answering him. "…Because the Empire's weapons are better in quality than Natra's?"

"That's one part of the answer. But ours aren't particularly bad. It's just that military powerhouses are bound to have weapons of higher quality. Anything else?"

"There's more? Um…" She frowned in concentration but was at a loss for an answer, finally giving Wein a perplexed look.

The sight was so charming, it brought a small smile to his lips.

"I can't go around telling everyone this, but the purchases are my way of apology to the Empire. Natra got more than its fair share in our transaction the other day."

"Really? But everyone's always praising you, Wein. They say you took down the Imperial ambassador a peg or two," she bragged, as if she'd done it herself.

He shook his head. "In diplomacy, it's no good if something's one-sided. Especially when you're negotiating with a nation more powerful than you. You want to avoid creating any unnecessary ill will. This is the second reason."

She nodded but then tilted her head questioningly. "And the third reason?"

"Ah, that's—," started Wein.

"Pardon me!"

A messenger came flying into the pavilion, yelling so loud that anyone present could hear. "The Kingdom of Marden is advancing on us!"

Falanya's eyes flew open.

"They've finally made their move," Raklum whispered to himself.

And Wein avowed in a voice of indifference, "—because we'll be needing to use them immediately."

The Kingdom of Marden was directly to the west of Natra.

Though neighboring countries, their official relations were virtually nonexistent, limited to mostly private interactions. This was because Natra's politics and ideology followed those of the East, even though it was in the center of the continent. This meant they didn't have stellar relations with Western countries.

The two states were comparable in size, which was quite small. Their military strength was much the same—or rather, used to be. That was no longer the case.

The scales had tilted in favor of Marden ever since it had discovered a gold mine, leading it to emerge as a major power over the course of a few short years. On top of that, the mine was infuriatingly close to Natra's borders. Wein couldn't stand it. Oh, how he'd internally screamed and cursed at it.

DAMMIIIIIT!

He'd seriously considered invading Marden once before, but in the end, the idea had fizzled away into nothing.

Now, Marden was trying to invade them.

It'd been decades since Natra had last gone to war with another country. In fact, there were quite a few soldiers without any experience outside of drills and keeping order within the nation.

Under the circumstances, it was natural for anyone involved to be ready to pack their bags and run for the hills—but that wasn't the case. As they gathered in a room at the royal court, Wein and his military commanders showed no signs of backing down.

"Just as you predicted."

"We are impressed by your foresight, Your Highness."

They kept calm for one reason: Wein had already foreseen that Marden would invade in the near future and took proactive measures with his commanding officers.

"It wasn't so difficult." He wasn't feigning modesty. It was the truth.

The current king of Marden had a truly poor reputation. The rumors of his violent reign of terror had even reached ears in Natra. This king had apparently surrounded himself with corrupt officials who turned a blind eye to his failures as a ruler, and then he kept banishing any who dared to speak out against him.

His behavior was setting the stage for a vicious cycle that would drive the country to ruin. With everything that had happened, even the gold mine was relegated to paying off major financial losses instead of contributing to the country's well-being. With fond memories of their previous, more competent ruler in their hearts, the people were full of dissatisfaction and disappointment.

Considering Marden's current state, the current conditions in Natra must have seemed like a once-in-a-lifetime opportunity. The Imperial army was no longer a nuisance now that they had gone home after their nation had fallen from power. This was the best chance Marden had to bring home a straightforward win. Everyone understood the appeal of glory and the spoils of war.

Of course, this was all under the assumption they'd win—but Natra had prepared extensively to prevent that from happening.

"What about the garrisons at the border?"

"They're avoiding battle and focusing on observing the enemy, as you instructed."

"Very good. Well, what are we facing?"

"According to reports, they're coming with a force of seven thousand," one of Wein's commanders commented.

"Less than ten thousand, eh? That was my most conservative estimate."

"They must be wary of Kavalinu. That country is home to a hot-blooded bunch, after all."

The Kingdom of Kavalinu was another country that directly bordered Marden. Like Natra, it also enviously eyed Marden's rich ore deposits. Thanks to the constant threat of foreign invasion by its neighbors, Marden had to strike a delicate balance between offensive and defensive forces. This was a perennial issue among warring nations.

"We have six thousand soldiers prepared to engage the enemy. It seems we've fallen slightly short," said another commander.

"We'll be fine. Our weaponry and armor are in order, I take it?"

"Yes. As expected, the Empire's equipment is all finely crafted. Marden stands no chance."

Because they'd anticipated this attack, the war council was doing nothing more than hammering out details and making small, last-minute decisions.

Wein let his mind drift elsewhere as he listened to them chatter among themselves.

We're well prepared. Luckily, we'll be able to wrap this up before the Empire causes us additional headaches.

Natra's fast track to subordination had been interrupted. As rumor had it, the Imperial Court was more preoccupied over which of the three Imperial princes would inherit the throne. Apparently, the divisions had worsened to the point that the various Imperial factions were on the brink of a civil war.

But Wein still recognized the Empire as a powerful nation. The foundation of the Empire hadn't been broken, and he was certain they would overcome this hardship, maintaining their position as the leading power in the East.

It was only a matter of time until he would have another chance to sell his country to the Empire. Until then, his job was to bolster power within Natra. After all, the more valuable his kingdom, the greater its price. In that sense, his actions would determine how much he'd be able to enjoy his early retirement.

Our soldiers have been trained to the Empire's standards. This war's perfect for proving our strength and value. It'll also keep other countries in check. Though it comes down to whether we can win—

Wein and the others had drilled the soldiers, studied the geography, refined their strategy, and even collected intelligence on Marden's army. There wasn't the slightest chance of failure. At the very least, Wein was confident the soldiers would be able to repel the attack, opening the option of a quick reconciliation.

It was obvious the Kingdom of Marden was looking down on Natra, figuring this would be an easy victory. They wouldn't come calling like this just to steal a plot of barren land.

It's perfect...!

His former deal with the Empire had resulted in a pileup of unfortunate coincidences that caused his last scheme to fall through, but that had been nothing but a stroke of bad luck. This time, Wein predicted everything would go according to plan. He indulged himself with a jolly little victory dance in his mind.

If Ninym were around, she'd have advised him to be more aware of his surroundings. If she did, he might've noticed something unexpected brewing under the composed faces of his commanders.

To be frank, the Kingdom of Natra's army was in a pitiful state before Wein's ascension to the regency. It wasn't that the king disregarded his army, but for a long time, Natra simply wasn't involved in any warfare, and chances for the military to prove its worth were few and far between.

It was only natural that the military's standing in the royal court suffered during these times, and it only got worse when foreign troops sauntered into the kingdom acting as if they owned the place. The shame the kingdom's soldiers endured was intense.

It was from this point that Wein had turned things around for them. Not only had he persuaded the Empire to train them, but once an opportunity came, he also chased the Imperial troops out of Natra lands. He'd even helped the army procure weapons from the Empire.

Of course, they were well aware that Wein's goal was to earn their goodwill, especially considering the kingdom's recent political unrest. Even with this knowledge, the soldiers and officers were grateful for everything he did, more so than he'd ever imagined—and their devotion was well beyond the call of duty.

It was at this point that Marden launched its invasion.

"Let us fulfill our duty as the swords of Natra!"

"If we cannot meet His Highness's expectations, then what sort of vassals are we, huh?!"

Their collective energy had boiled over and finally reached its peak.

Meanwhile, Wein remained as composed as ever—because he believed victory was assured—even though it was his first battle. The commanders knew it would be impertinent to keep shouting and cheering in front of him, so they settled down and forced themselves to at least seem calm on the surface.

No one showed their true emotion, which meant no one could've realized the massive gap in their expectations:

Let us bring glory and victory to His Highness!

Hurry up and get this over with! Retreat and reconcile!

Their intentions were mismatched.

The battle with Marden loomed on the horizon.

The Polta Wasteland was near Natra's western border.

As the name suggested, it was a barren plot with nothing but sand and rocks, especially in the early spring. There was no snow now, unlike in the dead of winter, when it transformed into a dazzling world of silver.

At the moment, seven thousand Marden soldiers were marching through the region under the strict command of General Urgio. He was a man in his prime with harsh features and an even sharper gaze. He resembled a bird of prey.

"Hmph. It's just as they say. There's absolutely nothing here," he grumbled from the top of his horse. "Those court pigs are incompetent beyond help. What's the point of seizing this place?"

"I bet they're just desperate to have us distract the masses from their failures," suggested the adjutant with a dry smile.

Urgio let out an ugly little snort. "In that case, they should distribute the cost of this campaign to the people instead. That'd be a much simpler way to pull the wool over their eyes. If these fools don't even understand that much, we've screwed ourselves by having them run our kingdom."

"If they did that, those talentless hacks would go too far and end up giving away our very livelihoods."

"We'll roast those pigs whole if that ever happens. I doubt they'd be worth eating, though."

As the two laughed bitterly, a soldier rushed up to them on horseback.

"I have a message! The Kingdom of Natra's troops have been spotted twenty-five miles to the east! They're advancing on us!"

"Ngh..." The general's eyes flashed.

"It seems they move quicker than we thought."

"Hmph. As expected of northern opportunists. They're quick. I give them that much. That is, if they didn't leave their spears at home in a hurry."

"But, General, I heard their soldiers have recently been trained by the Empire. If we let our guard down, it may come back to bite us."

"Eh, don't worry. They're about to find out firsthand that even if you teach a chicken how a hawk flies, it'll always be nothing but a chicken. Move our men faster. Since their troops are in a hurry to put their necks on the chopping block, we're going to finish this up right away."

"Yes, sir!" The adjutant began barking out orders.

Giving him a sidelong glance, Urgio turned his attention toward the east, reminding himself that he'd been appointed commander of this war—the reason why didn't matter. Natra was hardly a worthy enemy, but a victory was still a victory. He'd make sure to serve up their heads on a platter.

"Those weaklings better entertain me a little."

He was eager to soak this desolate land with the blood of his enemies and gave a nasty grin to no one in particular.

Meanwhile, Natra army leaders were reviewing intel about the Marden troops again.

"Just what we expected."

"Yes. Let's move forward with our plan and advance to the hill," agreed a mounted, elderly commander, nodding at Wein, who was reading a map on his own horse.

He was Hagal, the general of the Natra troops in the field.

Technically, the supreme commander of the army was Wein, but he had no interest in military exploits. The last thing he wanted was to steal credit for the victory from his officers, so ideally, he would've preferred sitting this entire thing out.

That said, this was their nation's first war in a long time. There was no saying what might happen. He prudently suggested accompanying the troops—in case they needed him to massage out a diplomatic solution instead. That way, if the opportunity presented itself, he could pacify their opponents and bring the whole incident to an end as quickly as possible.

Nonetheless, his soldiers were uneasy that he was nominally in charge. After all, he'd never set foot on a battlefield, and now he was leading an entire army.

This was why Hagal was the one truly in command. He was originally a high-ranking officer of a foreign military—renowned for his long military career and involvement in countless historic battles. It was quite curious how someone of his caliber was stuck in the backwater of Natra. But he had his reasons.

Threatened by Hagal's brilliance and popularity, a lord of his previous land attempted to have him killed a few decades ago. Fleeing as far as he could, Hagal eventually wound up in Wein's country.

Though the aging commander had recently stopped leading from the front, Wein know no one in their right mind would complain with Hagal in charge.

But, man, the military is a serious money-eating enterprise. Bye-bye, cash. Good-bye, funds.

With Hagal giving out orders to the army, Wein was relegated to a spectator role. Not that he had any complaints. He was treating this as a good chance to inspect the variety and quantity of goods consumed by the soldiers. This was the moment he'd realized exactly how much money it cost to mobilize his troops.

First and foremost, he had to pay them a salary. Then he needed to provide water and other provisions as well. On top of that, there were still the costs of the horses, their fodder, weapons, armor, and a mountain of day-to-day necessities.

After he added in sundry expenses and calculated the total amount it'd cost by the time they returned home, he nearly let out a harrowing moan. *Ugaaaaah.*

"Is everything all right, Your Highness?"

"Ah, yeah, yep... I was just wondering how fast we can put an end to this war."

That was the only way to stop them from losing any more money. He'd heard of kings who relished war, but he figured they must be pretty terrible at math.

"What do you think, Hagal?"

"It'll be difficult. War is a hard thing to predict before it actually begins... I take it you're hoping to make this a quick battle."

"I believe that'd be for the best—but there'd be no point in aiming for that if it'll cost us victory. What I mean is... Yes, what I want is to be convinced. Even if it takes some time, I want a result that convinces me this battle was a good use of our time. What do you think, Hagal?"

"Please leave it to me." The old man bowed reverently to the boy, who was young enough to be his grandson. "I vow this battle will be to your satisfaction."

"Let's hope for the best. Well, looks like we're almost there." Wein gazed ahead at the low hill as it came into view.

Six thousand soldiers fighting for Natra.

Seven thousand for Marden.

Across a barren wasteland strewn with rock and sand, the two armies faced each other. Though there was still quite a distance between the two hosts, the atmosphere of battle had already settled onto the scene.

From here on out, many men would be trying their best to kill one another.

"Your Highness, the troops are ready."

From a tent on top of a hill, Wein nodded at Hagal. "And what about the Marden army?"

"It appears they're prepared as well."

"I guess all that's left is to wait for the battle to start."

"Yes, indeed. Would Your Highness say a few words to everyone before they set out?"

"I don't mind, but is this really the time for a speech? I mean, will it *do* anything, Hagal?"

"Of course. A battlefield is the domain of death itself. In such a place, our hearts wear out faster than our bodies. A few words of encouragement will help keep them from breaking."

Wein couldn't argue with a seasoned commander. Besides, if he showed concern for the well-being of his men, it'd also lower the chance of a coup later on. But what should he say? As he continued to think, he walked over to stand in front of the entire army at the foot of the hill.

As he gazed over them, he made his decision: "Torace of Heinoy."

It was someone's name. In the center of their formation, one of the soldiers' heads snapped up. He was surprised and confused to hear the crown prince call him by his name.

"Your spear. It's upside down," Wein remarked.

"Wha...? Oh." The soldier looked down at his own hand.

Sure enough, the tip was sticking into the ground, and the wrong end faced up toward the sky. He fumbled, flipping his spear around, and quickly stood at attention again. By then, his face was beet red.

Someone burst into laughter, and it quickly spread across the army.

"Karlmann, Patess, Livi, Logli, it's not that funny," said Wein, piercing right through the din with his sharp warning.

The four names belonged to soldiers who were guffawing especially hard, and they shut their mouths with a start. This turned out to be just as comical, but the soldiers kept silent and limited the mirth to their quivering shoulders, knowing they might be called out if they laughed again.

Seems like they've managed to relax a little.

When he had observed them earlier, Wein had noticed they were tense. It was understandable. After all, it was the first time most of them would participate in a battle. Drills could help to a certain extent, but there were some things that had to be learned through real-life experience.

In any case, Wein had cleared the first hurdle. All that was left was to boost their morale.

"To this very day, people have called the army of Natra weak. To be fair, that was once true. And right now, those soldiers from Marden are looking down on us in the exact same way." His voice boomed, echoing through the crowd. "But I know how you've endured soul-crushing training. I know each and every one of you has courage beyond compare. And I know that as you stand here to face those invaders, there is nothing but fire in your hearts. You have no reason to believe you're weak anymore."

The relaxed atmosphere from earlier was gone. Now, the soldiers were impetuous, seized by a fiery spirit.

Fanning the flames he had set, he shouted out to them, "This battle is where we show them that we are the dragons of the north! Let it ring throughout the continent: *We* are the greatest army to stalk the land! Let us conquer all! We will rewrite history—today!"

"*YEAAAAAAAAAAH!*" Their collective cries shook heaven and earth.

It seemed he somehow managed to succeed.

As he let out an internal sigh of relief, Hagal rode up to him. "You were magnificent, Your Highness. I couldn't have sparked such fire in them."

"At the very least, they won't drop their weapons in fear," Wein replied with a slight smile.

"Did you plant some soldiers you knew in the crowd?"

"Don't be stupid. I was totally improvising."

"And you happened to know their names?"

"Well, I memorized most of them. It's not like we have hundreds of thousands of soldiers. If you add up the entire army, it comes to only ten thousand men."

"......" A perplexed look spread across Hagal's face.

As the feverish cries of their enemy reached his ears, Urgio clicked his tongue in annoyance.

"Ranting and raving like the opportunist scum they are," he spat.

"General, our preparations are complete."

"Good."

He squashed his irritation back down before facing his men, knowing he couldn't put his short temper on full display with thousands of eyes on him.

"Listen up, warriors of Marden!" he blared, voice rumbling in the pit of his soldiers' stomachs. "That over there is our pathetic little enemy! They've mistaken recklessness as courage and wish to oppose our advance! But no matter how many peasants they gather to make their ragtag army, there's no way they will ever win against us!"

Urgio sharply drew out his sword, and the soldiers raised their weapons to the sky.

"Crush them underfoot! We will soak this wasteland with their blood! Troops! Forward march—!"

Howling up at the sky, seven thousand men stomped on the ground as one united front.

"So they're here."

Their enemy advanced—a human tsunami. Wein could feel their presence overpower him from his position at the headquarters.

"Troops, stand ready!" barked Hagal.

At his command, the army raised their shields and spears. With the Marden on the offense, the soldiers fighting for Natra were forced to take on the defense: ready to stand in place and beat them back.

If Marden was a tsunami, then Natra was a levee.

The rival army steadily approached them. The tension was palpable, setting their skin alight and seemingly whipping the very air around them.

Natra would win this battle. Victory was certain. But fear was a part of human nature.

Wein watched the encroaching army with feigned composure, desperately praying inside all the while.

Please—let this go well.

The two armies drew closer. The distance between them shrank. His heart raced faster and faster.

Until finally, the tsunami hit the levee—

""——Huh?""

Wein and Urgio couldn't believe their eyes.

Whoa… Whoa, whoa, whoa…!

W-wait…?!

From their respective places, they gazed at the scene unfolding in front of them, united in a single thought: *What in the world is going on…?!*

On the battlefield, the soldiers of Natra were in a rather standard formation: From a bird's-eye view, you'd see them in a rectangular shape spread out before the Marden army.

Their opponents had their own battle arrangement. Their men were concentrated in the middle of its formation, unlike their opponent's uniform structure. The Marden were banking on breaking through the opposing center line, then turning around and destroying them in one go.

Humans are particularly vulnerable to attacks from the side and from behind. This principle can be applied to an entire army, too, meaning assaults from the rear are extremely advantageous.

To counter these attacks, the troops of Natra needed to focus on destroying the enemy soldiers in the center. That said, they were going against seven thousand men with an army of six thousand. If strength was in numbers, it was obvious which one had the advantage.

But war isn't determined by that alone.

After all, victory depended on many unquantifiable factors, like skill.

"General Urgio! We have a request for backup from the left flank—Loshina Unit!"

"A message has come in! The Sanse Unit has been annihilated! The Tljii Unit is heading there as backup!"

"General, the right flank's struggling as well!"

News from the battlefield hit them as one report after another came in: All reported the dire condition of the Marden army.

"No way…" Surprise spilled from Urgio's lips in spite of himself.

But his words reflected the collective bewilderment of the Marden officers.

How the hell are their soldiers this strong…?!

Wait, Marden is weak as shhhiiiiiiit?!

While Urgio and his staff were stiff with shock, Wein sat on the opposite side of the battlefield in disbelief.

What is this?! Huh?! Why are we beating the crap out of them?!

His words were no lie. The battle was completely one-sided.

The Natra and Marden men met in a zealous clash, but it was immediately evident which one was stronger—even before the impact of their initial collision died down.

The Marden troops brandished their weapons, single-mindedly focused on taking down the enemy in front of them. But their attacks weren't coordinated or collaborative: It was every man for himself.

But Wein's soldiers were different.

When Marden troops rushed in, some defenders raised their shields to stop the enemy assault, freeing up nearby allies to beat the attack back. On the other hand, when the enemy closed up their formation in self-defense, the Natra soldiers coordinated to break through it—all the while maintaining formation. Instead of fighting individually, the Natra army moved as one, with each soldier supporting the men beside him.

Though fewer in numbers, it was painfully clear that Natra had the overwhelming superior force.

"What's the matter, Your Highness?" Hagal questioned, noticing his confusion.

"…I was surprised. We're better than I thought."

Not that he doubted they'd win, but this was well beyond his expectations.

"Did you know it'd turn out like this, Hagal?"

"Why, yes. After all, we all invent and refine things to fulfill a need. To illustrate my point, the Empire has a long history of battles. This is one of the reasons they're able to train their soldiers so effectively. To be honest, even I was impressed when I observed their methods. Once we learned their ways, I knew we'd easily defeat a small country with nothing but minor skirmishes under its belt." He broke into a wry smile. "But I'm a little surprised by how weak they are. It's possible this is a setup, but I really don't believe that to be the case by this point. But, Your Highness…"

"Yeah, I haven't forgotten. We'll just have to whittle 'em down while we still can…"

Just then, a huge shout erupted from the right flank. After halting the Marden advance, Natra soldiers had gone on the attack.

"Looks like Raklum has made his move."

Roars and screams blared out of the crowd at the edge of the right flank.

Through strewn bodies and followed by the metallic scent of fresh blood, Raklum rode on his horse. Under his command, the officers spat out orders:

"Don't break formation! Move together as a unit!"

"Shore up the defense! Dispatch reinforcements!"

"The Marden are gettin' cold feet! Force 'em back!"

The soldiers at the front lines followed their instructions with a keen awareness that this battle was going in their favor, just as Wein had observed.

They were fighting well, and it was already affecting the enemy. In fact, the Natra soldiers were quickly overwhelming the enemy. Months of harsh training under the Empire's tutelage were coming to fruition, and as the battle wore on, the men's morale continued to rise. Thanks to Raklum's commanding officers giving out precise orders and the soldiers speedily carrying them out, they were pushing back Marden more and more.

Right now, their army was in the zone. They no longer felt any doubt.

This was why the commanding officers made a proposal to their leader, Raklum.

"Commander Raklum, sir! This is our chance! Let's launch a full-on attack!"

"At this point, we can smash through their defenses and take 'em from the rear!"

"Commander Raklum!"

Suggestion after suggestion whizzed past the captain's ears, but his eyes were cast downward. He was unresponsive.

The commanders looked at one another. This was different from the Raklum they knew, the one who matter-of-factly issued orders during their drills. They'd never seen this side of him.

One of them nervously reached out, wondering what was wrong. "Captain…?"

As he gingerly touched his shoulder, Raklum's head snapped up. The commander stiffened in an instant.

Raklum had been crying.

Grown men shouldn't cry—but tears poured from his eyes, heedless of his subordinates' gaze.

"C-Commander Raklum, what in the world...?"

"UWAAAAAAAAAAAAAAAAAGHHH!" blared Raklum in an agonizing, throaty voice.

This inhuman cry startled the Natra and Marden troops in the right flank, causing them to shake involuntarily and stop their movements.

They all turned toward the direction of the noise—Raklum.

"I... I'm sad," he admitted. With all eyes on him, he moved his horse forward. "This is the very first battle of the glorious Prince Regent Wein Salema Arbalest... His first step of many on a brilliant journey... and yet...and yet..."

The tears transformed into unbridled fury, blazing out of his shy eyes.

The Marden soldiers shivered at the sight of his rage.

"What worthless trash... All we're doing is clearing out weeds. It shouldn't be like this... We should be offering up the blood of strong, cunning, renowned prey, worthy of His Highness's splendor..."

Raklum suddenly dropped down from his horse and stomped across to the enemy, sauntering as though walking through an empty field. He finally came to a halt in front of the Marden soldiers, who were all frozen in place.

This was an unusual sight: an enemy leader standing before them alone, crying. It left them so dumbfounded, they didn't dare move.

"Your Highness... Oh, please forgive your retainer for his unworthiness."

Both of Raklum's long arms lashed out, flashing through the air like whips.

With a loud *pop*, a soldier's face split into two, and his body was callously tossed in the air.

"—At the very least, I vow to create a mountain of their dirty corpses."

With that, everyone came to their senses.

"K-kill him—!"

"Follow Commander Raklum!"

Raklum swung his gauntleted fist as the Marden soldiers swarmed him.

"He's pushing back the enemy! Their defeat is close at hand!"

Wein nodded in satisfaction at the messenger's report.

He goes a little wild sometimes, but it looks like it'll be okay this time. Good, good.

By handpicking Raklum as one of his officers, Wein had made the man unimaginably loyal to him. In truth, Wein had been a little concerned as to whether that might make things worse in a real battle. But considering how things were going, he figured everything would work out.

What the hell was he thinking, getting off his horse and bashing people himself? he'd come to think in hindsight over the coming days as detailed reports filtered in. Not that he had any way of knowing that at the moment.

But this is bad.

One after another, the messengers reported that they were at a major advantage. However, clouds of doubt continued to swirl inside his conscience.

Marden should just hurry up and cut their losses. If they don't...

As Wein fretted, Hagal's eyes glinted shrewdly. "Your Highness, our threads have begun to fray," he reported.

Gah. Wein narrowly escaped saying that out loud, hurriedly swallowing it down. "You're sure?"

"Yes... The battle conditions are changing again. Please prepare yourself, Your Highness."

Wein gave a short nod as he looked on at the battlefield and remembered what Hagal had said before they had set off for battle.

"Wait, our soldiers won't last long?"

"That's correct," Hagal had said frankly at the war council meeting.

"By training hard, our soldiers are almost unrecognizable in strength and likely to dominate at the start of battle. But they'll wear out after ninety minutes."

"Why?"

"Because most of them are unfamiliar with war," Hagal had explained. "The cold air, spilled blood and sinew, uncontrollable bloodlust… In battle, the heart gets worn down faster than the body. When that happens, your vision narrows and your ears start to close. This makes soldiers slow to come to the aid of their comrades or obey new orders. You could say it reduces the strength of our army by half."

"Even after all their training?"

"No amount of training can change this," he had said, nodding. "There are just too many things on the battlefield you cannot know unless you experience them yourself."

"…So Marden has the upper hand in this regard. Their experience might consist mostly of smaller skirmishes, but they've experienced war before."

"Yes. Unless their leader's exceedingly foolish, he won't overlook this opportunity. That means the deciding factor is how much you can whittle down their army until then."

"Let's hope he's the dumbest, most unaware leader possible," Wein had wished with a sigh.

But of course, his wish didn't come true.

—The enemy is moving with less force! Almost immediately, Urgio sensed this sudden change.

"General!"

"I know! Give me ten seconds!"

At the start of battle, they had seven thousand of their men fighting against six thousand enemy soldiers. But despite their early advantage, they currently stood five thousand to five thousand—an even playing field.

With the Natra army's movements slowing down, there was a chance to make a comeback.

But it was useless. That alone wouldn't be enough. If the Marden army couldn't beat them before sunset, their opponents would start to prepare for their next move, rest, and recuperate, meaning Urgio's men would have to fight them all over again.

This is our chance. Now or never. We'll have to—

This is bad.

On the other side, Wein's patience was wearing thin. The reason wasn't just the deteriorating condition of his army. It was because he'd pretty much hand-fed the Marden a way to turn things around.

It'd take time to prepare a counterattack. If the enemy started to move in before then—

I'm begging you not to notice…!

Wein sent a prayer to the heavens above.

But his prayers were in vain, for Urgio surveyed the battlefield and quickly spotted the epicenter of this change.

Are the front lines wearing thin…?

Though the Natra army was holding out and trying to keep formation, their center was weakening.

Why? The answer quickly sprang to mind.

To destroy the left flank of Urgio's army, Natra had shifted soldiers from the middle of their formation to their right. Unfortunately, their manpower slowly petered out before they could follow through on the attack, and they'd entered a stalemate and a thin formation.

An image of victory flashed in front of him. They could do it.

This is the moment of truth, he screamed in his mind.

"Tell the leaders on both flanks to keep whatever enemy troops they're fighting occupied—get the main forces back in formation!" he blared. "We attack as soon as everything's ready!"

"Yes, sir! What's the target?!"

"Isn't it obvious?" Urgio looked into the distance as his eyes gleamed. "The head of their dear leader!"

Ugh, crap—hold on! We're not freakin' ready yet—

The center of the Marden formation had unleashed an attack on his men.

The single blow targeted their cavalry, taking a huge bite out of their weakened army.

But the Marden forces couldn't be stopped. They pressed through the gap, worming their way through. There were no soldiers left to defend this opening on Natra's side. And with men fervently fighting on both flanks, Wein couldn't ask his troops to return to their original positions and block the new enemy advance.

Their opponents would burst through their main defense. There were about a thousand soldiers pushing through. When that happened, the only ones available for defense would be Wein, Hagal, and a hundred other guards on top of the hill.

"Your Highness, we must pull back. Quickly."

"I know."

There was only one path. Under Hagal's order, Wein and the others hastily made their retreat.

"General! He's escaping from their main headquarters!"

"How pathetic! He should just take the loss like a man. But there aren't that many of them up with him! Go after him on horseback! Have the infantry hold their main forces in place!"

"Yes, sir!"

Urgio divided his infantry. He set out after Wein with a cavalry detachment four hundred strong. They launched upward toward the top of the hill and skidded to a halt near their main headquarters, seizing a few craggy mountains behind the hill. Hiding in one of the shadows was the prince's personal guard.

"So you planned to run and hide again… Pity. Your heavy armor backfired on you!" he barked.

The guards in their enemy's headquarters were nearly all foot soldiers equipped with spears and shields. They couldn't outrun horses.

"Get them before they hide in the cliffs! Let's go—!"

He issued the order and descended the hill with his cavalry. As they closed the distance between them, the guards stopped moving and turned around in what seemed like resignation, forming a line of defense to face the coming attack.

But it was much too thin. They could be broken in a single charge.

Urgio raised a war cry, certain of victory—

"I told you not to come," cursed Wein in a low voice no one could hear. Then he issued a command. "All right, let's wrap this up…!"

Ninym Ralei ordered the soldiers, "—Archers, loose."

From the top of the cliffs, a sea of arrows rained down on the Marden army.

"—Ambassador! Terrible news!" Fyshe's door to her home flung open as her aide dashed in.

Fyshe glanced up from the reports on the battle between Natra and Marden. "Why are you so flustered?!"

"It's about the crown prince! I've obtained some documents! You won't believe what I've found! Feast your eyes on this!"

Fyshe caught the pages the aide thrust at her.

"Ambassador, didn't you mention something was missing when you looked into the crown prince? I think this could be the answer!"

As Fyshe scanned the papers in front of her and listened to the excited, blubbering cries of her aide, her eyes widened in surprise. "He attended the military academy...?!"

"Yes! He studied at the Empire's military academy for two years!"

Disbelief raged in her mind. But it was the truth. This evidence was undeniable.

"Our academy is full of national secrets. Why was the royalty of a nonvassal nation...?"

"I don't know the details, but it seems he hid his title and passed himself off as a commoner. Though his teachers may have been aware..."

"How did he get admitted?"

"It seems a high Flahm official in the Empire recommended him. It could be because the Kingdom of Natra is famous for accepting his kind long before other lands. Even though he held a position of power within the Empire, he must have been predisposed to helping the royal family in Natra for their role in protecting his people."

It seemed likely. The Flahm had an unbreakable bond. But there was something else Fyshe wasn't satisfied with.

"But why was this information omitted? I mean, I suppose it might cause some problems, but it's nothing too major."

"That's not all. Please read on."

Pressed by her aide, Fyshe turned to the next page of the document. It was two years' worth of test scores.

"This is..." She couldn't believe her eyes.

Literature, history, math, fencing, military history... Every exam had excellent marks, taken by someone at the top of their class. The name was blacked out.

"It was already censored when I received it. It seems the name was intentionally redacted."

Why would someone do such a thing?

The answer came to her in a flash.

"We have the reason right here," Fyshe explained. "It was to hide the

disgraceful fact that a foreigner—let alone a royal—was at the top of the class instead of a person from the Empire…!"

This was just unthinkable. How could something so foolish happen?

The Empire had created and nurtured an enemy—and now the claw it had created was pointed at its throat. And that claw's name was…

"Wein Salema Arbalest…!"

Below them, the Marden troops were on the brink of destruction.

They might have been lauded as a strong army, but many of their men were ready to flee in the face of a surprise attack. How could anyone remain calm when assailed by a shower of arrows?

Well, if there was anyone, it would be well-trained commanding officers and soldiers, experienced in battle and ready to rush in to defend their leader. There were a few men swarming their general at that very moment.

Because of this, Ninym easily spotted him from her high vantage point.

"Archers, continue to hit the remaining enemy soldiers. Cavalry, we're off."

"Understood!"

At Ninym's command, the cavalry charged down the hill all at once. The Marden troops were confused and helpless without their leader, and the Natra picked them off one after the other.

"It's going well, Captain!"

"Of course. That was the plan," Ninym responded coolly as she recalled how she'd arrived here in the first place.

"—Hide the troops?"

"Yep."

It was a few weeks before Marden would begin their invasion, and

Wein had just requested Ninym carry out a very specific plan in the meeting room.

"They'll be attacking us soon. According to my estimations, we'll be meeting each other right here in the Polta Wasteland." He pointed at a map spread out on the desk. "It's dotted with mountains and hills, an ideal place to hide soldiers. Keep them there and launch a surprise attack when the time comes. I want you to command them for me, Ninym. I'm already discussing it with my men."

"...I have a number of questions." She raised her hand. "First, are you absolutely certain when they'll attack?"

"The reports from my spies confirm it. There's no question they'll attack within the month."

"How many soldiers will we hide?"

"Pick those you trust the most—maybe seven hundred to a thousand. It'll be hard to hide a force any bigger than that. And it'll tip off the enemy if they see we have noticeably less manpower."

"Okay, so just enough to carry out an attack."

"Yeah. Lure out the enemy and attack from the side... That's our best method, though it depends on how the battle plays out."

"What about departing together? My soldiers can travel a bit faster to hide ourselves."

"That won't work. There are probably a few enemy spies in our troops, so if we divide the army in two later on, they'll rat us out. Then the attack will come to nothing," he reasoned.

She nodded and saw no issues so far. But she was most concerned about something else.

"Last question: Why me?"

"Huh?! Can our Miss Ninym not handle this?! You're always going around acting so high-and-mighty, looking like you can do just about anything, but I see! So you can't do it! ...Ah, Stop, stop, ow, ow—"

"Be serious."

"Okay, okay, I get it. Stop twisting my fingers already!" Wein shouted, yanking his hand out of her grasp. "It's simple. To pull this off, I need the right leader. After all, we need to keep a thousand soldiers hidden for a month. But if I assign one of my more competent leaders, it'll hinder management of the main forces. And there's always the possibly the Marden would get suspicious if a big shot military leader wasn't around for the big battle. That's why you're commanding them: No one will see you as a military threat, right?"

"True."

To the public, she was Wein's aide and a civil official. No one knew she'd trained to lead an army. But the troops would treat her with a degree of respect, knowing her family had served the royals for generations.

"Well, basically, I don't really trust anyone except you and Raklum. Those other guys made a vow of loyalty to my father and the country—not me. This is still a very delicate issue. I can't assign these tasks to just any old officer."

"The other vassals think highly of you, you know."

"Nope, no way! If I'm careless for even a *second*, there's gonna be a *coup*! History has all but proved that!"

His paranoia of enemies in plain sight made her shake her head internally. At this rate, it'll be a long way off until they could build a bridge of trust between Wein and the other officials.

"Well, if it really looks like you can't do it, I still have other ways of going myself… I'm sure you can handle government affairs while I'm gone."

"I won't…let that happen. If you're not here, Wein, who will take command of the main army?"

"Ah, well, I intended to put Hagal in command from the very start. I don't want to throw water on the soldiers' long-awaited chance at glory."

"…Is this really all right?"

"Don't worry, old man Hagal is, like, ridiculously strong. Yerp.

No need to worry. He's especially insane on the battlefield. If I went head-to-head with him, I'd hightail it out of there—but that's a separate conversation."

Ninym nodded, returning to the issue at hand. "If that's what you want, I guess I have to accept. Very well. I'll take the soldiers and lie in wait."

"I'm counting on you. Er, well, there's about a fifty-fifty shot we'll actually need you. As for me, I'd like to win, but not by *too* much."

"You don't want total surrender?"

"That kind of victory comes with its own problems… Well, there's no way that'll happen, so it doesn't matter too much. Let's hurry up and get started."

Ninym nodded, calculating in the back of her head. She needed to choose and prepare an appropriate hideout, soldiers, and foodstuffs. There was plenty to do, all under a veil of secrecy, but she indulged herself in vocalizing one last fear.

"By the way…will you get any work done without me?"

Wein grinned. "Oh, it'll be hell when you get back."

…Just how much work did he put off?

She smiled bitterly, charging on horseback with her subordinates. They were aiming for a group of ten Marden soldiers attempting a retreat. In the center of the small unit was their leader—Urgio.

"Th-the enemy is coming!"

"Protect the general! Hold the line!"

They quickly gathered into a defensive position.

"—Your line is too thin," Ninym noted.

With her at the forefront, the cavalry shot through their defenses and dashed in, routing any retreating Marden soldiers. Without breaking stride, they swung toward the center of the formation, facing Urgio with his brandished sword.

She cut off his arm as they raced past each other.

Spraying blood, he fell from his horse.

©Falmaro

"G-GWAAAAAAAAH…!" he howled in anguish.

Turning her horse around, she gazed down at him as a ring of her men defended her. "You're the leader, aren't you?"

Soaked in his own sweat and blood, Urgio looked up as he writhed in agony, sweating. "Th-that voice…and that white hair…"

"Surrender. You can still be saved if you get immediate medical treatment," she advised.

But that sent Urgio into a blinding rage. "Surrender… Surrender, you say…?! Don't screw with me!" he howled.

Warm blood poured from the gaping wound in Urgio's arm, and he breathed heavily, on the verge of death.

"I'm the general of the Marden army! Do you think I'll submit to a woman, much less some ashy slave?!"

"I see." She swung her blade and, with one smooth motion, sliced through his neck.

His head thudded onto the ground.

"Raise his head and spread the news. The enemy has been defeated… And do not let his dying words leave your mouths."

"Understood: The enemy leader was silent up to his final moments."

"Very well, then."

The adjutant raised the bloodied head and gave a hoot of victory.

Their soldiers answered with a long war cry as the Marden troops fell silent, finally defeated.

Ninym's eyes slipped past them, shifting her attention to the shadows of the mountain. There stood the soldiers from headquarters, those who'd lured out Urgio and his troops. Ninym turned toward the boy in the center of it all and gave a big wave.

"It seems to have gone well, Your Highness."

"Sure looks like it."

The Marden army fell out of formation, like clumps of baby spiders. The loss of their general robbed them of the will to resist any longer.

Though he'd suggested the surprise attack, it was beyond Wein's expectations that they'd be able to successfully draw out and defeat the enemy leader.

"So I guess this battle's pretty much decided?"

Hagal nodded. "Because their general was defeated behind the hill, their main troops on the other side aren't aware the war is over. We must quickly spread the news of our safety and their leader's death. Once we do so, they'll retreat."

"Got it. Let's get going, then."

"Yes, Your Highness."

The men began to move under Hagal's command.

Afterward, Wein joined Ninym and her troops and returned to the top of the hill, where they witnessed the news spreading: The prince had returned, and the Marden leader was dead. This gave heart to the Natra soldiers and soured their enemy's morale.

With many of Urgio's commanding officers killed and no one left to unite them, the Marden scrambled to their feet and scampered away.

In a little less than a day, the troops of Natra were the victors in this battle in the Polta Wasteland. Each and every soldier swelled with triumph, drunk on the strongest liquor of all—glory.

Well, all except one.

Sooooo what the hell do I do now…?

Wein was the only one thinking about the future—and the only one filled with dread.

"Aghhhhhhhhhhh…" Sprawled out across his desk, Wein made a big show of exhaling the gloomiest, ghastliest sigh he could manage.

Ninym was standing beside him. Back from the battlefield, they weren't wearing armor anymore.

Normally, she pushed Wein in some way or another to get work done whenever he slacked off, but today was different.

"…This could be a problem," she whispered.

Wein wasn't the only one frowning. Ninym's eyebrows were furrowed, too.

"I finally understand what you were trying to say before I left," she whispered.

As he looked quizzically at her, she reminded him of the other day. "You told me it wasn't a good idea to win by too much."

"We should launch a counterattack!" shouted a commanding officer, giving voice to the thoughts of everyone else in the meeting room. "Marden attacked us first. Now that we defeated them, their eastern region is wide open! We can seize a huge swathe of their territory!"

It was the night after their decisive victory in the Polta Wasteland. The war council gathered to decide on a new objective moving forward, and the officers all had lofty ambitions.

"I agree. Our soldiers sustained minimal damage. And because we won in such a short period of time, we won't run out of resources anytime soon."

"We've also gathered the provisions Marden left behind. Our soldiers' stomachs might actually explode from eating *too* much."

The war council roared with laughter.

They were all relaxed, giddy and joking after their recent success. It could even be said that they were getting cocky, but it was understandable: They'd been considered outcasts for decades. Now they were basking in victory and glory. These officers were only human, after all.

On top of that, they had been on the defense this time, meaning their victory wasn't very sweet. War was largely synonymous with gaining territory or goods, so it made sense that they'd wanted to escalate to considering invasion.

However, there was one person who didn't share this sentiment.

Quit screwing aroooooooound! Seated at the head of the table, Wein was in a mood that was the polar opposite of the others. *Marching out without a solid game plan is* way *too risky!*

The Polta Wasteland was within their territory, so they had a detailed map of it. They could study how the roads connected, the layout of rivers and mountains, the general terrain, and where nearby towns and villages were located beforehand. This preparation facilitated their advances and allowed them to make trips to replenish their supplies.

However, that wouldn't be the case inside Marden. While the war council was armed with a simple map of enemy territory, its precision was worlds away from the one of their own country. They would have to face phantom villages, unpassably deep rivers with unknown tides, roads that had fallen into disrepair, etc. These were all within the realm of possibility.

While a lone traveler could probably make the journey somehow or other, it would cost too much time and effort for a group of thousands to make a wrong turn. Not to mention, if they didn't make enough progress, their morale would fall. It was very likely their missions to replenish supplies would be delayed, or their resources would run out altogether. Meanwhile, the Marden army would have fresh, well-provisioned troops ready to go. It was an all-around bad idea.

But I can't say that noooooooow!

If there had been obvious losses to both sides in the last battle, the commanding officers would have readily agreed to Wein's request. But he'd look spineless and totally clueless about the art of war if he was to suggest conservative action now. There was no doubt their loyalty would come crashing down like an avalanche. Next stop: coup.

I've got to have someone else stop them...!

He was desperate, but he couldn't have Ninym do it. Even now, she was right behind him taking notes, but she was only his aide, after all. Though he'd temporarily put her in charge of his subordinates, what he needed at the moment was on an entirely different playing field. And she had no power to speak here.

That left only one candidate. Wein looked at Raklum sitting a few seats away. *Raklum! Hey, psst, Raklum!* he tried his very best to communicate with telepathy.

Raklum noticed Wein, who was about to bore a hole into him from staring so intently. He responded with a look: *Yes, what is it?*

Wein pleaded with his eyes. *This war council's headed down a bad road. Jump in and somehow calm them down!* his eyes said.

...I see. Please consider the message received, Your Highness, Raklum's eyes replied.

Fortunately, Raklum was adept at reading minds.

"Commander Raklum, may we ask for your thoughts?"

I'm begging you! Wein's eyes silently yelled.

Please leave it to me, Raklum's eyes reassured. He gave a small nod and spoke. "No time to rest. We have no choice but to attack immediately!"

Not even clooooooose, you freakin' idiot!

Wein mentally tackled Raklum.

Why the hell are you on their side?! Stop smilin' at me! God, I swear I can hear your thoughts. "I did it, Your Highness!" I'm cutting your next paycheck, ya spineless pushover!

The officers were all caught up in the potential of an invasion. Even if Wein objected, there was just no way he could reverse this. No, that was absolutely not an option. But there was another approach.

I didn't want to have to do this, but no use whining about it now!

"Everyone, I understand your opinions," Wein affirmed.

The officers in the room stopped moving. The air that had been stirring a moment before was now still. All eyes turned on him.

"Hagal," Wein called out to the old man sitting next to him. "Now that we've won, you understand how everyone might be pushing to exploit this opportunity. But seeing as I have no experience, it's difficult for me to determine whether we should march forward despite lacking a definitive plan or if that'll ultimately be too much of a burden on the soldiers. I want to hear your professional opinion."

"Understood..." Hagal nodded reverently. "Our stamina wears thin all too quickly. Once the lingering taste of victory is gone, our men will find themselves heavy with fatigue. When that happens, they'll still be able to make the return trip home, but their knees will give out if we command them to immediately mount an invasion—especially one with no real goal."

"Hmph..."

"Ngh..."

Looks of sour displeasure appeared on the commanding officers' faces, one by one. After all, someone just stopped their exciting new plan in its tracks. But they knew better than to carelessly defy Hagal, who had far more experience on the battlefield than they did.

Everything's going good so far—!

Wein could feel the officers starting to waver and introduced a new question to support his case. "Well then, should we consider withdrawing?"

It would have been nice if Hagal said they could, but it was unlikely. And as Wein predicted, the old man shook his head.

"There's no doubt this is a golden opportunity. We'd be fools to let it pass us by... That said, we can't invade without aim or strategy. It's of utmost importance that we fully understand our soldiers' physical and mental limitations, then focus on a clear target."

"...Any objections?" Wein asked.

The commanding officers said nothing.

"Excellent. I have one proposal as an offshoot of Hagal's opinion." Through squinted eyes, he carefully examined the map spread out on the table. "As you know, this area is not 'blessed' with much of anything, by any means. But we can say the same exact thing about Marden as a whole. In fact, eastern Marden has very few places of strategic merit. Based on our military strength, if there's any location worth storming—"

He jabbed a spot on the map: Marden's eastern mountains. It never held much value until recent years, when it became one of their most valuable assets.

"—it's the Jilaat gold mine. If we're going to target anything, it's this."

A loud commotion tore through the room. Everyone turned to face him with outwardly confused expressions, but on the inside, Wein smiled at this 180-degree reversal of events.

That's it. That's the reaction I was looking for. No matter how you go about it, going after the gold mine is totally illogical!

It wasn't an exaggeration to call the gold mine a national treasure. In fact, it might have been more important than the royal capital. Wein hadn't researched it in detail, but there was no questioning the tight security measures Marden must have put in place. Accepting a proposal to attack the mine would force the Natra army to invade a place without sufficient intel—while still reeling from the aftereffects of the last battle. It didn't matter if it was theoretically a good strategic move. Such an attack was the height of recklessness, wastefulness, and impulsivity.

Of course, Wein knew all this. He brought up this plan to make his audience consider the fact that the advance itself might be meaningless.

The officers were thinking something along these lines:

The gold mine's impossible. If we're gonna attack, it has to be somewhere else. But where? Are there any other places in the eastern sector just as valuable?

Nope. Nope, there aren't. There's nothing but the gold mine.

After this grand suggestion, the alternatives paled in comparison. Even if they managed to capture a small fort or village, wouldn't it be worthless compared with a gold mine? When they realized that, Wein knew for sure that would deflate his commanding officers and their eagerness to invade.

This is gonna lower their opinion of me somewhat, but it's not so illogical that they can't forgive me for making this mistake! That's a price I'm willing to pay—as long as we withdraw.

Everything was going according to plan. In his mind, Wein was already striking a victory pose.

"…Your Highness," interjected one of the officers with a stern look. Wein suspected he was racking his brain, trying to figure out how to convince Wein that his plan was ridiculously reckless. Not wanting his subordinate to lose face, Wein considered how best to seem as though he was very impressed by the officer's inevitable admonition for his foolish plan when—"I am in awe of your intellect."

"Huh?" Wein blinked in surprise at these completely unexpected words.

"The Jilaat gold mine… Yes, it's exactly as His Highness says. We should make this our target," another one agreed.

"I must say, I'm utterly amazed—to think His Highness had discerned that we'd been secretly planning to take the Jilaat gold mine for ages!" confessed another.

"Huh?"

"According to the latest reports, the gold mine is in a vulnerable state. There are fewer than a thousand soldiers stationed there. We're already verifying the route the troops will take."

"There's no such thing as certainty in war, but this is worth the risk."

"While we've been celebrating our victory, His Highness had the good sense to weigh the actual feasibility of putting a plan into action. As your vassal, I am humbled."

"Go on, Your Highness. Give us the order to march!"

"Let us go attack the Jilaat gold mine!"

"Long live the prince!"

"Long live the prince!"

"Long live the prince!"

"……"

…*Ninym, help.*

She calmly smiled. *Sorry, no can do.*

And that was how the Kingdom of Natra decided it would launch an attack on Marden.

"We would've been able to stop them if we'd won by anything less than overwhelming victory…," Wein moaned lazily.

"If I'd been able to capture the enemy leader instead of kill him, we could have held postwar discussions or requested a way to reconcile our differences… I'm sorry, Wein," she apologized.

"I mean, he rejected your offer to surrender, didn't he? Don't worry about it."

"…You're right."

"The real problem is the next step. First, we make sure the intelligence on the gold mine isn't a ploy," he started.

"And then review our supply lines and maintain the soldiers' morale as best we can," she continued.

"In the grand finale, we steal the gold mine before Marden has a chance to stop us."

Easier said than done.

Though they'd come up with appropriate steps, this would be their second battle, back-to-back. They'd trip up at some point. But that might give everyone a dose of reality and be enough reason to withdraw. At least, that was Wein's line of thinking, and Ninym was on the same page.

—Or that was supposed to be the plan.

"We ended up capturing it, huh?"

"We did, indeed."

The two turned their heads to look outside the window.

Against the dark backdrop of glittering stars, a large shadow pierced the heavens: the Jilaat gold mine. It'd been Marden's main source of income, but now it was occupied by Natra. Ninym and Wein were currently in a room of a residence at the foot of the mine.

"…Had no idea the guards would be total wimps," he offered.

"They were surprisingly weak… They ran away after one minor attack."

"The people running this place must have embezzled some money out of their budget. Their king should really keep his eye on these things…"

"Yeah. That aside, we have to think about what to do next."

"Yeah, I guess so…"

Together, Wein and Ninym groaned at their growing list of problems.

Anyone who mentioned Elythro Palace in the Kingdom of Marden to anyone would hear the same thing: It had been built as a physical testament to Marden's newfound wealth.

King Fyshtarre was so pleased with this extra income that he ordered the palace to be built by the most renowned craftsmen from the most luxurious materials in the world. He liberally poured a river of cash into its construction. Everyone expected it to be a magnificent palace, destined to go down in history.

Unfortunately, there was one bad apple mixed in this group of first-rate craftsmen, resources, and funds. That was the hopeless anomaly of a third-rate king.

It's said everyone has at least one good trait. It was still a mystery which of King Fyshtarre's traits could be considered "good," but as this incident would come to show, it *definitely* didn't lie in the arts.

With his absolute political authority, the king stuffed his amateurish knowledge of architecture—as nonexistent as some crumbling old coin—and questionable aesthetic into a blueprint and proudly thrust it at the craftsmen in charge.

The artisans took his childishly simple designs and combined all their skill and persuasion to pacify the king. They managed to change it into something presentable, at the very least. And while they weren't necessarily proud of the final result, they had certainly proved their talent to their peers.

That said, even the most talented artists have a limit to what they can achieve. The final layout made it difficult for people to come and go, the interior design was terribly mismatched, and there was a general lack of uniformity in its furnishings. Anyone with even the slightest intellect could tell it was both functionally and aesthetically lacking.

The only saving grace was that King Fyshtarre wasn't the sharpest tool in the shed and that his servants were wise enough not to point out any of these deficiencies. He was an emperor with no clothes, contently and obliviously reclining on his garish throne inside his perfect palace.

But this peaceful scene would disappear just a few days later.

"This is bad; oh, what a mess…," muttered a voice down the hallway.

Everyone agreed the western corridor of Elythro Palace was pointlessly long. Through this excessively lengthy path, a man in his prime briskly hurried forward.

He was round. Like, roly-poly round. His legs were short, and his arms were, too. His face was round, his belly was round, and he looked as if he would roll around nicely if you punted him.

His name was Jiva. He was a diplomat of the Kingdom of Marden and one of the country's very few long-standing retainers.

"I've got to hurry…!" Mumbling over and over to himself, Jiva finally arrived at the reception hall with a pale face.

The entire room was intricately designed—from the corners of the walls to the shadows of the pillars. It was conspicuously extravagant even by Elythro Palace standards. And of course, it was King Fyshtarre's favorite room, meaning this was where they had all their morning meetings. The emergency meeting on this day was no different.

"What's the meaning of this?!" roared a voice, reverberating through the hall and paralyzing those it reached. "Those insects of Natra have gone and *stolen* the Jilaat gold mine?!"

A long table was set in the center of the room, where Marden's chief retainers gathered around it. In the middle of it, the king of Marden, Fyshtarre, was beet red, jeering at them. He was impressively obese. Jiva's physique may have run in his family, but the king was fat because he'd removed the word *moderation* from his vocabulary.

Right now, anything in his field of vision had the potential of becoming the next target of his rage. Jiva's appearance belied a cleverness that he put to good use: He continued through the shadows of the pillars and knelt behind someone's chair.

"Master Midan, sorry I'm late...!"

This elderly man was known as Midan, the minister of foreign affairs. In other words, Jiva's superior.

"You must have been very busy to be late, Jiva."

"I'm terribly sorry. My meeting with the ambassador ran long."

"Hmph. You've heard, haven't you?"

"Yes...," Jiva replied.

"Good. Stand back for now."

Following his orders, Jiva bowed and placed himself in a corner of the hall.

The next voice that rang through the hall wasn't King Fyshtarre's, oddly enough.

"My king, your anger is justified."

It was the voice of the man sitting nearby King Fyshtarre—Holonyeh. It might have been difficult to imagine from his hunched back, withered frame, and eerie, twisted smile, but he was the minister of finance.

Tch, backstabber... Jiva mentally clicked his tongue.

Whenever the minister opened his mouth, he gave off an unpleasantness that didn't just affect Jiva. In fact, the faces of most people in the room soured and scrunched.

"At this rate, the situation will only continue to deteriorate... We must quickly draw up plans on how to deal with this."

"That's a rather self-important thing to say," Midan spoke up. "Lord Holonyeh, the management of the gold mine, including its security, was entrusted entirely to you. It hardly seems appropriate for you to make such remarks, especially after we've been robbed of a crucial resource... Do you intend to obfuscate your responsibility for what's happened?"

The daunting glint in Midan's eyes would've stopped anyone younger and less experienced in their tracks. He wasn't about to forgive anyone who tried to smooth talk their way out of trouble. But Holonyeh was equally formidable and not in the least perturbed.

"It would be wrong to say it was stolen without a fight, Lord Midan. According to the reports, each of the guards valiantly accepted Natra's challenge and fulfilled their duty."

"Then how was it stolen?"

Holonyeh gave an uncanny smile. "Yes, yes, but alas, if only General Urgio hadn't been defeated so easily. Then this wouldn't have happened." He switched gears and feigned ignorance. "Come to think of it, I believe the trueborn Mahdia are the ones in charge of appointing generals. You know, I think they were the ones who recommended General Urgio. Honestly, those who are good-for-nothing always cause others trouble. Wouldn't you agree?"

"Why you..."

To backtrack, the current retainers serving the Marden hailed from two different factions.

The first was the Mahdia, the one Jiva belonged to—people born in Marden, raised in Marden, and chosen to serve Marden. Of course, internal discord was present within the group, but as a whole, they were unflinchingly loyal to their kingdom.

The second faction was the Stella. They were born elsewhere but allowed to take positions of power due to their skills and talents. Overall, their loyalty to the nation was weak, as they were mostly lured to the country by a high salary.

In recent years, the friction between the two groups had grown increasingly malicious. Before then, the number of Stella was too low for them to organize themselves into a faction.

As to what caused this rapid change—indeed, it was the discovery of the gold mine. Ever since, the royal palace had been turned upside down. Until then, Marden had been a poor, insignificant little country. They'd gotten used to getting by on limited funds, but the goddess of good fortune paid them an unexpected visit. Not a single person understood why.

That was about the same time a group of sharp-eyed foreign bureaucrats appeared, with Holonyeh at the helm. They brought their experience and success of managing government affairs in other nations, telling King Fyshtarre they could put his sudden windfall to good use.

But these sly old foxes were better versed in stirring up political conflict, and duping the nervous country bumpkin of a king was more than easy. He appointed each of these newcomers to a high-ranking position one by one, and they wielded their power to their full potential. Their management of the gold mine maximized profits and pleased King Fyshtarre so much that he put even more foreigners in positions of power.

Of course, this didn't amuse the Mahdia in the slightest as the influence of the Stella grew more and more each day.

For the Stella, the others were an eyesore, placing such importance on being native-born. With this, their factional fighting had already gone past the point of no return.

"Oh, why did we have to let the Mahdia have their way back then?" Holonyeh continued. "You know none of this would've happened if we'd left it to General Draghwood, don't you? From my perspective as a loyal retainer and patriot of Marden, it's nothing short of a disgrace."

"You're saying you're one of the nation's '*loyal* retainers'?"

"Of course. I'm proud to say there's no one with more respect and affection for our king and country than myself."

Upon deciding they'd send troops to Natra, the two factions had bitterly opposed each other over who was better suited to lead: Urgio the Mahdia or Draghwood the Stella. In the end, it was the Mahdia who'd snatched the post, but now it seemed to have backfired.

This is so stupid. Jiva sighed inwardly.

While he was indeed one of the Mahdia, he kept his distance from any political squabbles. It disgusted him to no end that everyone was willing to disregard the best interest of the country for the benefit of their own faction.

"Enough of this pointless yapping!" blared Fyshtarre to break up the glaring contest between Holonyeh and Midan. "I shall tear apart any deserters who've shamelessly come running back home with my own two hands. But our focus right now is the gold mine. Holonyeh, you have a plan, don't you?"

"Yes, of course. It's no grand scheme. We lost the battle thanks to General Urgio's personal folly. I believe the next battle is best left to General Draghwood."

"Wait," Midan immediately cut in. "It's true General Urgio underestimated Natra, which led to our downfall. But isn't it reckless to assume a mere change in leadership will solve all our problems? Particularly if the enemy soldiers decide to hole up in the mine, an average-strength force won't be—"

"In that case, let's prepare three times as many soldiers than the last battle. It should be enough to crush them."

"You fool! That'd mean neglecting our borders! You can't be so oblivious you haven't realized Kavalinu is targeting us from right next door!"

"That's precisely why. The gold mine is of utmost importance to our country. We'll weaken if we spend too much time getting it back, making it all the easier for Kavalinu to prey upon us. We have no choice but to take it back at once, before neighboring countries have a chance to involve themselves… Unless you have another plan, Lord Midan?"

Midan looked away and turned toward Fyshtarre with a proposal. "Your Royal Majesty, I believe we should consider a diplomatic solution with Natra."

"…Are you suggesting I sit down with those insolent, invading dogs?" Fyshtarre's face darkened.

Midan boldly continued. "First, it'll take us some time simply to mobilize a large force. Even after we complete the mobilization, it's not clear whether we'll be able to immediately retake the mine. If we prolong our war against Natra, our resources will deplete, which will create an opportunity for our neighbors to strike us. By speaking with Natra and negotiating with them to get the mine back, we'd reach a much faster and safer…"

"It is you who are foolish," mocked Holonyeh. "Anyone who knows the value of that gold mine wouldn't dare let it go."

"…By possessing the mine, Natra will become the target of other countries. On top of that, Natra will need to manage the day-to-day functions of the mine to have any hope of extracting value from it, which is beyond the capabilities of a small nation with limited human resources. Even *you* realize that, don't you?"

"Hmph…" Holonyeh hesitated slightly, but he promptly shook his head. "But even if Natra agrees to this, their price will be proportionate to the mine's value, right?"

"There should be room for negotiation… Your Royal Majesty, please leave this matter to me."

After hearing the proposals of his two retainers, Fyshtarre closed his eyes, gravely considering his two options. He then locked his eyes on Holonyeh.

"…Holonyeh, call for General Draghwood. We'll gather soldiers to launch a strike."

"Yes, Your Royal Majesty."

"Your Royal Majesty…!" pleaded Midan.

The king gave Midan, who still refused to back down, a perfunctory glance. "If you're so set on discussing this matter with them, go there and prove it to me... You've got until the moment my troops depart to reach a diplomatic solution."

"...Sire!"

After they'd taken some time to iron out the details, the meeting was adjourned. As the nobles exited the hall, Jiva knelt by Midan's side.

"You heard, didn't you, Jiva?"

"Yes."

"Start gathering information and head toward the gold mine. Make them give it back to us no matter what. We must avoid anything else that may discredit the Mahdia."

"......"

"Jiva?"

"...Understood. I will see to it."

It went without saying he had his own thoughts on the matter, but this was a part of his job. Besides, even he agreed it'd be too risky to mobilize such a large army.

But how much can I actually do in such a short period...?

But Jiva set off on his task even as he felt anxiety filling his chest and weighing him down.

Ninym Ralei was early to rise from bed. It was part of her morning routine to wake up at the crack of dawn. After all, she lived in an era when daylight was too precious to waste.

Plus, she was participating in a military expedition and needed to avoid squandering lamp oils and candles. That made starting work at sunrise the most optimal solution.

But the very first thing she did was cleanse herself.

"...Phew."

It'd been one week since Natra took over the Jilaat gold mine.

The Natran forces had put the former managers of the mine back to work and had familiarized themselves with the layout of their temporary headquarters, finally bringing their affairs up to speed. At long last, she could take some time to shower.

Well, seeing how she was out here, she used the term *showering* pretty liberally. She couldn't soak herself in hot water or dab scented oil on her skin. As a woman, she felt a keen desire for a few more luxuries that catered to her wants, but as a sensible aide, she drove it out and kept it at bay.

Well then, I better go wake him.

Stepping out of the bathtub, she dried off and dressed herself before continuing down the hallway to head for Wein's bedroom.

"Miss Aide. Up early again, I see." Two guards stood in front of his door.

"I can't oversleep, or His Highness will, too. Anything to report while you were on watch?"

"Nothing to report. All has been quiet."

"Very good. As you were."

The guards stepped away from the door, letting Ninym enter the prince's room.

It was modest. On the day their forces had seized this place, the army had appropriated everything of value in the building. The original owners had taken most of the valuables with them as they fled, so the army hadn't gathered much. But looking beyond material possessions, this room contained the Kingdom of Natra's second most precious item.

It was Wein Salema Arbalest, sleeping on the bed.

"...Wein," she breathed into his ear.

He wouldn't wake up. She knew that. He loved sleeping—and despised getting up. If she let him, he'd sleep, dead like a log, until the middle of the day. He'd wake up only when the sun shone through his windows a little *too* brightly.

Right now, the best she could do was open the curtains, let light pour in, and cheerfully whisper in his ear. Only then would he groggily crawl out from under his warm blanket.

But that wasn't her first course of action. She rested her hands on her chin by his pillow and stared at his sleeping face. Every now and then, she'd watch Wein sleep—it was her moment of indulgence.

"Mnn… Hrnnm."

He groaned, croaking incomprehensible noises from the back of his throat. What could he be dreaming about? He looked too peaceful to be caught in a nightmare.

Could he be dreaming about me?

She had no way of knowing, but the thought alone made her happy.

I think I'll make some of Wein's favorites for breakfast today.

Out here in Marden, they didn't have the luxury of full-time chefs or meal service, which left Ninym in charge of making all his meals. Her cooking skills and ingredients couldn't quite match those of the palace, but considering the circumstances, the dishes were relatively elaborate. As they should be. They were for the crown prince, after all.

Relishing in these thoughts, she heard Wein talking in his sleep as he broke into a relaxed smile. She caught a few of his garbled words: "Boobs…so big…so bouncy…"

"……" Ninym patted her own chest.

Well, they certainly couldn't be called "bouncy" by *any* stretch of the imagination. She made a mental note to give him a full-course breakfast of his least favorite things.

In hopes of calming her rage, she peeked again at his sleeping face.

His face looks…manlier somehow. She played with his bangs. *He's getting taller. We were the same height as kids, but he shot past me before I knew it. He's really filled out, too.*

For her part, there was a possibility her own growth spurt was at its end. Her features and body had assumed their womanly shape, acquiring just a touch of roundness. But let's make no mention of her breasts for now.

The relationship between the two hadn't changed from childhood.

Back then, they'd suddenly grab each other's shoulders and draw each other close, freely expose their chests, and engage in discussions about boobs. It had never mattered that they were opposite genders.

At times, she was happy to maintain this intimacy, but at others, she couldn't shake her doubts and fears. Whatever the emotion, Wein made her heart race every time, though she'd learned to expertly hide it under her cool exterior. But she wondered if he'd ever notice. It seemed unlikely.

Or he may have already noticed and acted this way on purpose.

She cursed him and considered drawing on his face for a second. But she quickly shook her head.

…I have to wake him up soon.

She stepped away and strode over to the curtains, pretending she'd just walked in the room. The light poured in, causing him to stir slightly.

"Wein, wake up. It's morning," she announced, knowing she'd no longer have him all to herself. He was all hers only in the cusp between night and day.

"—Now that it's ours, let's use the mine as much as we can," concluded Wein as he looked at it from his office window.

"Are you sure? Even though they'll fight us over it?" Ninym stood beside him, voicing her concerns.

It was possible for the gold mine to operate on its own. The miners and their families lived on-site. Aside from the initial confusion over Natra's military occupation, the troops ensured that peace and order quickly returned. It wouldn't be too difficult to convince them to cooperate.

Of course, Marden would come to take back the mine as soon as the last soldier was ready to fight. This gold mine was that vital. If the new and improved Marden army put their all into it, they'd undoubtedly be able to do some serious damage. But Wein had already included that in his calculations.

"They lost. It's a done deal. Giving it back now would cause morale and confidence in me as a leader to take a nosedive."

Ninym couldn't argue with that. "Then we'll need to prevent Marden from stealing it back."

"First, we learn the lay of the land. We've already done basic reconnaissance, but it's not enough. We'll need to know the mine inside out."

"I know it was kind of unavoidable, but it's unfortunate that we couldn't find any documents or information."

The guards of the mine had retreated quickly enough, but they'd either torched or run away with almost every record or document related to the mine. It must've been their emergency backup plan in the event of a crisis and surrender.

"Pardon me." There was a sudden knock at the door. Raklum stepped in. "Your Highness, I have reports regarding the progress of a number of investigations."

"Good work. Take it from the top."

"Yes, sir. On the whole, our relationship with the residents is improving, thanks to your support. We've distributed food and are in the middle of helping build proper homes."

"That's to be expected, especially if you consider the way they were treated prior to our arrival," said Ninym. Her manner of speaking instantly switched once Raklum entered the room.

The Natra army had kicked out the Marden garrison to gain control over the gold mine. Of course, the mine came with a residential district for the miners and their families. What they found were dilapidated huts crammed together and malnourished people within. It was obvious they were either slaves, traded for cheap, or offenders who'd been sent there to do hard labor. There were even people who were completely innocent of any crime who had been tossed in on the whims of those in power.

The work in the gold mines was notoriously intense. And of course, there was no decent food to speak of. Assuming there was anything close to a doctor was absurd. The houses were piles of scrap material that had been cobbled together, and most workers died after a few years. Learning of their plight, Wein made sure food was rationed and asked soldiers to build them simple shelters. The people of the mines unanimously expressed their appreciation.

It was all part of his plans. Sure, they were using up more resources, but the residents' cooperation was essential in order to extract gold. It'd be unwise to give them reason to riot or revolt when a clash with the Marden was just on the horizon.

Besides, that kind of inefficiency is a huge waste.

Death meant a loss of not only manpower but also knowledge and experience. Dismissing the miners as unimportant and letting them die without cause was a detriment to the mining industry.

"How's the map coming along?"

"The surrounding area should be surveyed within the next couple of days. However, the inner tunnels of the mine are expansive and will take some time to fully understand. We're working with the miners, but because the turnover rate was so incredibly high, finding someone with in-depth knowledge is…" Raklum trailed off.

"Understood. You can continue on as planned. Was that the only report?"

"Yes… Well, there is one other matter."

"What is it?"

"One of the mine residents is requesting a meeting with Your Highness."

Wein tilted his head curiously. "If it's about an appeal, I thought I left that to you."

"That's what I said, but he insisted on meeting Your Highness directly. I looked into his background, and it seems he's one of the mediators who represent the residents."

Wein and Ninym met eyes.

"What do you think?" Wein asked.

"I'm sensing a plot of some sort. It may be in your best interest to meet him," she replied.

"Sounds about right. Okay, Raklum, call 'im in."

"Yes!" Raklum ambled out of the room promptly.

He soon returned with a man, a gaunt figure without an ounce of strength left in his feeble body. Most of the residents were severely underweight, but this was something worse. He'd probably fall over with a light push.

…But that wasn't the only thing on Wein's mind as he looked upon the man kneeling before him.

"It's a pleasure to meet you, Your Highness. I am—"

"Pelynt."

The man's head snapped up, responding to his name.

"I saw a personal description of you when I was researching high officials of Marden. You look a lot different now, but there's no doubt it's you."

"…So the rumors about your intuition are true. I'm humbled." He bowed his head again. "My name is Pelynt. I served the royal palace of Marden until a few years ago."

"Were you bested in a political fight?"

"Ah yes. I see your insight knows no bounds. I was forced here after my fortune was stolen from me."

"So you're looking for a fresh start in my country?" Wein asked.

That was the only logical explanation, but to Wein's surprise, Pelynt shook his head.

"Yes, but that's not the reason I'm here today. I've prepared a gift, before I make my request… This is for you." Pelynt held out a weathered scroll.

Ninym acted as the middleman, presenting it to Wein, who inspected the contents.

His eyes swam over it in surprise. "This is…a map of the mine's interior!"

"Yes. It is a complete reproduction, with every single tunnel accounted for."

Wein would've given an arm and a leg for it. He'd need to confirm the details of the mine, but his next step would change as long as he had this.

"Why are you giving me this?"

"I thought it might be something Your Highness might need, so I stole it before it was burned."

"...I see. This is priceless." But that made Wein stiffen. What favor did this man have in mind? "Go on, Pelynt. What is it you want?"

"Yes, of course." He took a deep breath, gathering all the power in the pit of his stomach, and spoke. "—Please, I ask you not to forsake the people of the mine."

"...Wait, what?" Wein frowned at the unexpected words.

His bewilderment spread to both Ninym and Raklum, whose face in particular was pulled into an uncomfortable grimace.

"You shouldn't forget your manners, Pelynt," Raklum warned. "You can't possibly know the pains His Highness has gone through for your people. Don't you dare disregard that."

"That's precisely why I ask." Under Raklum's gaze, Pelynt continued without wavering. "With all due respect, I would've exchanged the map for money and left this place far behind me if His Highness were not so virtuous. But after seeing how nobly His Highness conducts himself, I knew I couldn't keep this a secret." He took out a bundle of papers.

"What are those?"

"Information on mining activity that I wrote down in secret. Please have a look."

As tension mounted in the room, Ninym delicately took the documents and passed them to Wein. He looked down. As Pelynt said, it was a record of the ore in the mine, apparently going back to the mine's earliest days. Wein continued reading.

As he neared the latest entry, he stopped. "…Hey, this can't be…"

"Yes. Those numbers are correct," divulged Pelynt solemnly. "The mine's drying up."

There was a small town not far from the Jilaat mine, a quiet place with not much in the way of industry or problems.

At least, it used to be. At the moment, it was the gathering point for soldiers from neighboring towns keeping a lookout for the Natra army. The air was tense, and security was tight. Those with means and connections took refuge far away, but others continued to live their lives on bated breath. Anyone openly traveling through the town was either an eccentric or under unique circumstances.

Jiva was surely the latter. He was staying in a room at an inn that'd seen some better days.

"—And that concludes my report on the mine residents."

"I see. You've done well."

Two men were in the room. One was the Marden diplomat, Jiva. The other was his personal spy. Jiva had sent him to Natra's base camp to feel out if they'd be willing to talk, while he ventured into town to set up the negotiating table. He received reports from the spy a few days later, but—he couldn't believe his ears.

"To think the people of the mine were treated so cruelly…"

The plain chair in the room creaked as Jiva hung his head. Sure, he'd heard the rumors that the miners were treated inhumanely, relentlessly used for what they're worth. But the mine had been fully entrusted to Holonyeh, and the Mahdia had never been able to question him, especially because he always turned a profit.

…No, that's not the only reason. They probably pulled the Mahdia's top brass over to their side.

On top of holding the country's purse strings, Holonyeh's men were skilled in instigating political strife. It wouldn't be difficult to cajole the

Mahdia when it came down to matters like this. And if the leadership kept quiet, the underlings would never get a chance to say a word. That was the position Jiva was in. As for those who tried to step outside the line—well, they naturally disappeared before getting very far.

"…You're sure Natra isn't forcing them to work, right?" Jiva confirmed.

"Yes. On the contrary. They're providing food and housing… With all due respect, sir, their hearts no longer belong to Marden."

"Yes, yes, I thought as much."

Of course they'd never have any loyalty to a country that essentially treated them like slaves. To the residents, Marden was a vicious ruler—and Natra, their liberator.

"Their crown prince… I've always heard he's a righteous and benevolent young man, but it seems the rumors are true. How are their troops looking?"

"It appears they're investigating the surrounding area to understand its geography. They've only laid the groundwork, but they've taken steps toward building a fortress."

"……"

Natra was getting ready to fight against Marden by fortifying their defenses. It wasn't possible to approach this lightly anymore. Jiva made a decision.

"I have no choice but to go speak with them as an emissary."

"That could be dangerous. As things stand, you could be killed."

"There won't be any progress if I can't overcome this much. Let's hope we can count on the prince's benevolence."

Determination in hand, Jiva began preparing for his journey to the gold mine.

Meanwhile, Wein gave a deathly moan and collapsed onto his desk. *"Uwaaaghh."*

It was hard to believe this was the same guy the Marden diplomat was giving such high praise.

"...Don't slack off. Come on, pull yourself together," Ninym said.

But her voice didn't carry its usual power or vigor. For once, her feelings were on the same page as Wein's.

"...It's drying up! Dry as bones! Yeah, yeah, just my luck. This *had* to happen right now. We came *all* the way over here, stole the mine, and went to freakin' *war* with Marden over it, then, right when we thought we've won, the whole thing turns to shit. Why's this happening to me...?"

Ever since he received the map, Wein had begun thoroughly investigating the authenticity of Pelynt's documents.

The results came back positive. There was no mistaking it: The gold mine was about to run out of ore. *Of course* he was in despair! If he was the only one involved, this could be laughed off with a slap on the knee. But that wasn't how national strategy worked. Who was going to forgive him with a whoopsie-daisy and a bop on the head for something of this magnitude?

"But we can't afford to sit around and do nothing," Ninym lamented, outwardly directing this at Wein but saying it to herself. "We have to decide what to do next."

"Yeah, we've got no choice but to withdraw, right?" Wein said sullenly, lifting his face slightly off the desk. "We fought because we thought this mine was worth *something*. That was the whole point of taking and defending it—to preserve its value. But now that it's not even worth a single gold piece? We're better off doing damage control and washing our hands of this place as quickly as possible."

It was logical. Even as they sat here discussing business, the army had running expenses to consider, and they were especially high due to being in enemy territory. The sooner they got out, the better.

"Then what about our promise? The one we made to Pelynt to look after his people?"

"He was only talking about *people*. He didn't mention the mine.

We'll just take anyone who wants to come along. I mean, our kingdom is a melting pot to begin with, built by people who had no other future. These guys aren't any different. Folding them into our mish-mosh country isn't going to upset anything."

"…That's true." She contemplated, nodding. "Should we inform the miners and prepare to withdraw?"

"…No, not yet."

"Why's that?"

"There's definitely gonna be some complaints if we back out now."

If he made the executive decision to genially hand this land back over, he'd certainly affect the army and the nation's pride. At the very least, they needed to come up with some kind of justification.

"Shouldn't we tell the troops the truth? If you're hell-bent on not telling everyone, maybe we can at least share it with the commanding officers?"

"Sooner or later, news will make its way down to the soldiers. Then their confidence in me will really tank. If we're not careful, some of 'em might take their anger out on the miners."

"So…we're lame ducks until Marden sends their army."

"Yeah, they'll send us a nice, big, fat group of soldiers to take back the mine. When our men see they're clearly stronger, we'll all agree to withdraw… I think."

Thanks to a growing list of surprises, twists, and turns, this half-baked plan was the best he could come up with.

"What about selling it to another country—without letting them know the mine is no good? Kavalinu, maybe?" Ninym suggested.

According to Pelynt, the mine had been entrusted to Holonyeh. As the documents passed through the hands of government officials, they each took care to report the profit slightly higher than it actually was so they could embezzle even more money. It was very possible Holonyeh himself didn't even know what was accurate at this point.

Meaning Pelynt, Wein, Ninym, and the others present at that previous meeting were the only ones who knew about the gold mine's dismal condition. They could sell it to another country in a standard case of adverse selection. It wasn't totally out of the realm of possibility.

"It won't be easy to get together and sort this out. There isn't enough time for that. And we'll have to go up against Marden if we take too long. If that happens, we can pretty much kiss any profit good-bye. And there's definitely gonna be some hard feelings if they ever find out."

It was a tough choice. It was hard to let go of the place they'd fought so hard for.

Where could we find a buyer for this sort of thing?

The gears in Wein's head started to turn, only to be suddenly interrupted by a commotion outside the building.

"I wonder what that could be?" Ninym asked.

Peeking outside the window together, he saw a group of soldiers hurriedly rushing back and forth. Just as he thought they were under an enemy attack, a knock came at the door.

"Apologies, Your Highness!" Slightly out of breath, Raklum appeared before them.

Wein immediately fired off his most urgent question. "Is the enemy attacking?"

"No."

Wein urged him to continue with a look. *Well, what is it?*

"It's an emissary. An emissary from Marden has arrived."

"——" Wein's eyes widened, but not because of the news.

He'd been hit with a sudden stroke of inspiration.

Raklum continued. "He's requesting a meeting with Your Highness. What shall we do?"

"...Did he give his name? What's he look like?"

"He said his name was Jiva, a diplomat from Marden. Based on his demeanor, there's no question he's a high-level government official."

"Sounds kind of familiar. You know him, Ninym?"

"Yes. I recall he's a member of the royal court."

"All right, Raklum, guide him to the reception room. I'll be there soon. Be on your best behavior."

"Understood!" Raklum promptly turned on his heel and lumbered out of the room.

"Ninym, I'd like you to make our guest feel comfortable."

"I'll see to it immedia—" She stopped midword upon seeing her master's expression. "What's wrong, Wein? You're making an odd face."

"Ah, no, it's all clear to me now."

"...What're you talking about?"

Wein grinned. "We've got a buyer for the mine."

Jiva was led to the reception room and waited patiently in a chair. At first glance, he might have appeared meditative, quietly sitting with his eyes closed, but a bit of nervousness surfaced onto his round face.

But this wasn't strange in the slightest. After all, from his point of view, he was in the middle of enemy territory. It was common for emissaries to be killed, even if they were sent to negotiate. There was a distinct possibility that armed soldiers were gathering outside the room at that very moment.

...But I think I'll be okay.

If they wanted to kill him, they would've already made their move. Plus, considering his status and the crown prince's alleged benevolence, they could probably have a discussion at the very least.

Reaching an agreement is going to be our biggest problem.

If anything was making him nervous now, that was it. He'd prioritized time and hardly researched his opponent. He knew only bits and pieces, and it wasn't clear if this was for better or worse.

As these worries filled his mind, the door swung open to reveal a girl with translucent white hair and red eyes. A Flahm. Come to think of it, he'd heard they were common in Natra.

"His Highness Prince Regent Wein has arrived."

A young boy stepped into the room following after her and accompanied by several guards.

"It is an honor to meet you, Your Highness," Jiva extolled, bowing reverently. "I am a diplomat of Marden, Jiva."

"And I'm the prince regent of the Kingdom of Natra, Wein Salema Arbalest."

He's so young.

Jiva had heard the prince was in his midteens, but he still had the look of an innocent child as he stood there in front of him. But his demeanor was dignified with the air of a proud leader. He wasn't some decoration or symbol or king due only to blood. Jiva wouldn't be forgetting that anytime soon.

"—First of all, please accept my most humble apologies for appearing unannounced, Your Highness," he began courteously.

They were facing each other across a desk. Ninym was taking notes behind Wein.

The prince responded diplomatically. "We understand that some problems require our immediate attention. Which is why I'd like to wholeheartedly welcome you for coming all the way here," he said, then shrugged his shoulders. "But it happened a little too quickly, so we weren't ready to receive any guests. My apologies. This was the only room available. I would have liked to prepare a more formal setting."

"Thank you for extending such hospitality to me, Your Highness. It was my own folly for not informing you earlier. Even if you greeted me in an empty field, I would be overcome with gratitude."

"I appreciate you saying that." Wein broke into a smile, as if talking to a close friend.

Jiva could see why the people of Natra loved him. But he wouldn't be swayed. After all, he was a man of Marden, and the battle between the two had just begun.

"So then, Lord Jiva, what has brought you to us today? You must know this territory isn't very friendly to Marden citizens at the moment."

There it was. The heart of the issue. Jiva gritted his teeth for a moment.

"Yes, of course," Jiva started. "In place of an army, I've come to express our appreciation. Thank you for taking on the responsibility of guarding this land. We are so grateful that you're willing to discuss how we can transfer the ownership of this gold mine back to us."

Upon hearing his words, Ninym and the guards gave the same speculative expression. *Say what?*

If he'd boldly ordered them to give back the mine, the soldiers would've been ready to end his life. Sure. But he said the last thing they expected to hear.

Even Wein was surprised by this turn of events. But here's what separated him from the rest.

"Hmm, yes, I seeeeee. Your mind is set."

While everyone stood there dumbfounded, Wein saw through his intentions in an instant.

Ninym scribbled down a question on a piece of paper. *Wein, what's going on?*

He's basically saying, "Let's pretend none of this happened." His writing was smooth, fluid.

She frowned for a few seconds, then realization dawned on her face. He gave her a secret little smirk.

Marden wanted the gold mine back as soon as possible. But any negotiating would undoubtedly drag on forever as they worked out reparations, exchanging prisoners of war, and redefining country borders, among other things, all while dancing around the topic of Marden's previous acts of aggression and violence toward Natra.

Looks like he's jumping right to the part where our countries forgive and forget. This tubby guy may not look it, but he pulls no punches.

It could also be a way of erasing the truth of their defeat, helping their prideful king Fyshtarre save face. It was a pretty brilliant move.

"There are no words to describe our gratitude for safeguarding this area from neighboring countries like Kavalinu. These enemies continue to threaten us from all sides. We would like to offer you a reward as an expression of our gratitude."

Of course, this so-called reward was nothing more than reparations and a buyout. There'd be some arguing over exactly how much it'd amount to in total, but so far, things were going more smoothly than your average postwar negotiation.

While this proposal seemed to cede more advantages to Marden, there were obvious merits for Natra as well.

"Ah, you've really saved us. This gold mine is our country's life force, you see. If it was stolen by a foreign power... Oh, we just might need to unleash our wrath and mercilessly destroy that enemy nation," Jiva said.

This was one such merit. Evading war with Marden was a pretty good deal.

Natra might've won the battle in the Polta Wasteland. But what about the next battle? And if they won again, the battle after that? When it came to their military strength, Natra was at an obvious disadvantage. At some point, their country would hit its limit. Even if they held out against Marden, another country would find an opportunity to attack.

Of course, Marden was dealing with the same problem—but Wein had some serious doubts as to whether King Fyshtarre could weigh the risks, even if he tried.

Fyshtarre is all about pride. No matter how many times he loses, he'll get back up again... Another defeat will just piss him off. Sorry, but I've got zero interest in going down together.

It wasn't such a bad idea to erase this battle from history. Without the shame of losing, there was a good chance their king would calm down for at least a while. In that time, Natra could use the money they swindled out of Marden and increase their military strength.

Well, there were some disadvantages, too. To start, their patriotism and price would be bruised. The troops would not be very happy to hear this, seeing that their battle honors would be redacted alongside the war itself. And if Marden compensated them monetarily, it'd leave a bad aftertaste in everyone's mouth. But there was still enough reason to accept Jiva's proposal.

It's basically confirmed... Marden has no idea the mine's drying up.

Only a few others knew the whole truth. If he continued to wait for another solution, his luck would run out eventually, meaning his men's confidence in him would plummet. On the other hand, it was obvious they'd be mad if the gold mine was sold to another country.

But what if they sold it back to Marden right now?

He could give it back before having a chance to profit from it. That meant he wouldn't be held accountable, even if the truth about the dwindling value of the mine was discovered. Instead, conflict would break out in Marden's inner circle.

And if Marden said they wanted a refund, Natra could feign ignorance. He'd initially lose the respect of his soldiers, but they might reevaluate his actions if they knew the truth.

This is my only chance to avoid war and swindle them out of a ton of money...

Are you going to go with his proposal? Ninym wrote.

Yeah, but if we take their bait too soon, they'll know we're hiding something. We gotta act unsure for a bit, Wein responded.

Don't get too greedy, she warned.

It'll be fine. I won't do anything to tip them off.

She gave him an uneasy look, but Wein just flashed a confident grin in return.

...I can't read him.

As far as Jiva was concerned, the proposal he offered was his last resort. If he had more time or a bit more generosity from King Fyshtarre, he could have found another way.

But this was the only way he could reconcile with any actual substance—and still satisfy his king. Jiva knew he'd been dominating the conversation, precisely because he understood it would be difficult to accept such a proposal. He was trying his best to smooth things over.

But could this ploy actually work?

Across from Jiva, the boy stared in silence. No words could faze Wein: His gaze bore straight into his opponent's eyes.

It's like hammering away at a steel sculpture with a wooden mallet... But I can't back down now...

No, he mustn't back down. Those were his feelings, but Jiva trembled in spite of himself. His journey to the mine was flickering before his mind's eye.

The people of the mine dressed in tatters.

The soldiers of Natra feeding them rations.

Once their troops were gone, what would happen to the residents? When the Marden returned to this territory, would they still be treated like humans?

...God! What am I thinking? We need to get back the gold mine. I need to do all I can to make that happen. This is going fine, just fine.

As Jiva reassured himself over and over, Wein started to stir. "—Livi."

Jiva wasn't sure he heard him correctly and looked on in confusion.

Wein continued. "Sefti, Regis, Talfia, Karaln..."

"Y-Your Highness... What are you saying?"

"Names," he explained coldly, his voice piercing through Jiva. "Names of my men who died in the Polta Wasteland."

"——" Jiva felt like his own heart might leap out of his chest.

What an unimaginably compassionate ruler! Many of his subjects held Wein in high regard. Jiva knew this.

"I hear your proposal. That might be one possible interpretation of this entire situation. But, Lord Jiva, in that case, where should the souls of my men rest? What should be marked on the graves of those who died serving their country?

"That's, ahhh..."

"You're not suggesting we write *Here lies some idiot who died in the Wasteland* on their graves—are you?"

Under Wein's steady gaze and kingly presence, Jiva was unable to form a coherent sentence.

Upon this sight, Wein cheered in his heart. *All right, it's working!* But Ninym appeared sullen.

Isn't it working too well? she wrote. *If this negotiation falls through, won't things end up as the opposite of what you want?*

Nah, this much is normal. Actually, I wanna give him just one more push, he scribbled back.

Fortunately, Wein could pass for a kind and generous ruler. He knew he could persuade Jiva if he mentioned his own soldiers and citizens. The more difficult he made the negotiation, the larger the gold on the other side.

"Lord Jiva, do you realize how the people here have been treated?"

"…Yes."

"Not too long ago, one of their representatives came to me with an appeal. He asked us not to abandon his people. He made this request to Natra, not Marden. You know what this means, right? It was enough for us to imagine the treatment they'd suffered under your hands. Suppose we returned the mine. What would become of these people? If you snatch away their last hope, they'll be left with only despair."

"……"

"With all that said, I'll ask you one more time: What brought you here, Lord Jiva?"

—Become someone noble.

Jiva suddenly remembered the words his mother used to say to him. It was a faint memory. He'd pushed it away to avoid looking back at the boy who'd been bullied. During that time, he did his best to keep his mouth shut until he could go home and pretend everything was fine. But his mother saw right through him.

—Become someone noble. Be someone your future self can be proud of.

These were the words that pierced his heart, and he'd made up his mind: He would live a life he wouldn't be ashamed to look back on in ten, twenty, thirty years.

That's how it should have been anyway.

But then he was faced with failure. Pressure. Self-preservation. Fighting.

Before he realized it, he'd lost touch of those childhood dreams and traveled down a path far from light.

That's just how it was. He'd made excuses, telling himself ideals were ideals *because* they were unattainable.

But the young prince was in a far more difficult position, and yet, he didn't hesitate or falter when it came to protecting his people.

"…Prince Wein."

"What?"

"Before I answer, I'd like you to allow me a single question."

"Very well." Wein's eyes didn't contain a glimmer of a doubt. They radiantly gazed forward.

"…The person standing behind you, Prince Wein. What is her relation to you?"

Jiva was thinking back to a memory of a young boy. He had the same translucent hair as the Flahm girl in front of him.

That boy had been a Flahm, too, and had been persecuted for it.

What made him think of that day now?

Jiva finally knew the answer.

"Ninym is my heart."

I wanted to be like him, Jiva thought.

What kind of question is that? ·

While Wein maintained his confident tone, Jiva's question made him cock his head in confusion. He tried to get a read on the diplomat, but Jiva had bowed his head, hiding his expression.

Wein and Ninym used it as a chance to pass a few more notes between themselves.

Maybe I'm a rare sight? Ninym suggested. *In the West, Flahm would never be present during diplomatic negotiations.*

Then he would have brought it up sooner or with more emotion, Wein replied.

True… Maybe he's impressed you don't discriminate between citizens, soldiers, or Flahm.

Ha-ha, so it's simply because this diplomat is so incredibly empathetic? No way that's the reason.

But if you're right, then he might not want to continue negotiating.

It'll be fine. If that happens, I'll eat a potato through my nose.

As Wein joked in an easygoing reply, Jiva quietly raised his head across the way.

"—Your Highness, I understand how your heart must feel." Jiva's expression was clearer, less burdened or weighed down by something. "Please forgive me for disrespecting those fallen in battle. It seems I've misunderstood."

"...Hmm?"

Wein felt something was off, but Jiva continued on. "There was blood spilled in your country's name. You've fought to claim this land for Natra. You're determined to protect the citizens. It is all too clear we must take up our bows and arrows."

"What?!"

"I imagine this will be my final job in Foreign Affairs. But I won't waste a minute in informing King Fyshtarre of your steadfastness."

"Wai—"

"Well then, Your Highness, I must make haste to the royal palace. Please allow me to say it was truly an honor to hear your personal anecdotes and exchange words with you." Jiva bowed deeply and hurriedly excused himself from the room.

Wein and Ninym stared until his back disappeared. They finally lifted their gaze, petrified for some time, and locked eyes.

"Um...Ninym?"

"... I'll go get the potato."

Those were her only words.

Ever since her big brother had headed to the west to lead his army, Falanya dedicated time out of her busy schedule to go onto her terrace and gaze in his direction every day.

She understood it was a silly, pointless thing to do. His letters were proof enough that he still hadn't returned. No matter how much she rubbed her eyes, she knew he wouldn't appear in front of her.

She understood in theory, not in practice.

Now that she thought about it, she'd done the same thing while he was studying in the Empire. Back then, she looked toward the east. If there was no one to interrupt her, she could continue to stare out forever. Truth be told, with the king bedridden and the prince gone, very few people could scold her for her actions.

"Princess, please return to your room. Too much wind is not good for the body."

One of those people, the chamberlain Holly, called from within, and Falanya turned to face a swarthy elderly woman of portly stature with short hair and dark skin.

It was uncommon to see those of her race—even in Natra. She was from the southern part of the continent, but Falanya didn't know the details. For as long as she could remember, this woman had taken care of her.

"Just a little while longer. I have to pray for his safety," Falanya said.

"Whether you're praying on a cold terrace or inside a warm room, I'm sure they'll be heard all the same."

"That's not true. I think God listens to the prayers of those who are suffering."

©Falmaro

"Then I believe God would say you should take care of yourself first. Besides, Princess, these hot, fresh pancakes may end up in *my* stomach if you're not careful."

"Oh dear, luring me in with food. What a dirty move, Holly."

"My god says it's a sin to let hot food go to waste." Holly laughed as she set the table, and the scent of pancakes subtly wafted out.

Falanya finally stepped in from the terrace.

"Nanaki," she called out toward the wall.

A boy emerged.

This was her guard, Nanaki. From his translucent white hair and red eyes, it was obvious he was a Flahm—just like Ninym.

"Let's eat together."

"……" Nanaki gave a slight nod and sat down with Falanya.

Holly divided the pancakes as she observed this delightful scene.

"Wein says he's doing well in his letters, but I wonder if it's really true," Falanya said.

"He isn't really the type of person to complain over small things, is he?"

Holly had long looked after Wein, too. His personality had gone through different phases, but she'd always thought he was the type of child who kept his weaknesses to himself.

"They have no problems," whispered Nanaki, devouring his share of the pancakes. "Ninym is with him."

Yes, Ninym Ralei. She was his trusted aide and confidant, and she was like a sister to Falanya.

"…Yes, Wein and Ninym have each other," she said.

She trusted Ninym almost as much as Wein. When they were together, it seemed as if there was nothing they couldn't do.

"Yes, you're very right. Why, with Wein and Ninym there, I could ask to join their military efforts, and—"

"No," whispered Nanaki.

"Absolutely not," scolded Holly.

Her dreams quickly dashed, Falanya melted across the desk.

"It's incredibly dangerous, and you don't have any time to spare right now, Princess. You said you were interested in studying politics, didn't you?"

"Well, yes, I suppose I did."

Though Falanya had been raised with the tenderest love and care, she'd recently started diving into her studies in order to help her brother. But when it came down to it, her studies were quick to become a bother and slow to come to fruition. She unconsciously moaned at each and every lecture.

"Ahhh... He must be facing challenges I can't even imagine, but I'm sure he's dealing with them just fine."

Falanya gave a small sigh as she thought of her brother galloping around the west.

As for how Wein was currently faring...

"*THIS SUUUUUUUUUUCKS!*"

He was in his room writhing in agony, a far cry from his sister's dignified image of him.

"I'm screwed, royally screwed. How could I have seriously thought I could get out of it that way...? Yeah, right... Ngaaaaaaah!"

"Told you your greed would backfire," scoffed Ninym coolly, her expression stern.

"Plus! Rumors are spreading like wildfire! Rumors about the very meeting we just had!"

"We never made the guards swear to secrecy..."

While Wein and Ninym had been preoccupied with their failure, the guards had passed everything that had transpired to the soldiers and residents of the mine.

The gist of the story was whittled down to: *Marden tried to solve everything with money, but the crown-prince regent firmly refused for the good of his army and the people.*

The guards who had already been full of adoration for Wein cast Marden as a treacherous, savage tribe and Wein as a kindhearted, sage ruler with an ear to the heavens.

Here are a few snippets from the residents and soldiers upon hearing the news:

"Damn Marden. How dare they insult those who gave their lives for their country. Nothin' but mindless beasts!"

"Even if they *could* deceive us with money, it'd never hide their vile hearts."

"Yeah, but we can always count on His Highness. Even when they offered enough gold to cover the national budget, he still shot 'em down."

"He's our national treasure. We can never sully a decision by His Highness!"

With that, the army's spirit ascended to new heights. The residents of the mine were moved to tears and unanimously expressed a desire to serve His Highness until the very end of their days.

"I'm guessing now would be a really bad time to withdraw... All I wanted to do was sell the mine and make lots of money. Why'd it have to turn out like this...?" Wein collapsed on the desk. *"Gwaaah."*

Ninym tried to console him. "...I think it's a good thing. That he turned you down, I mean."

"Whaaaa?! Miss Ninym, what part about any of this is *good*?! Get your head on straight! On top of being knee-deep in debt, the perfect chance slipped through my fingers. And you're *okay* with that?!"

"But it would've meant accepting the enemy's terms and wounding our soldiers' pride. If you think about it in the long term, it could have damaged your reign."

"Well, I'm not planning to be in charge for very long anyway! In fact, I plan on selling the country to the Empire the second I rise to the

throne, so— Owwwww?! Quit trying to stick a potato up my nose…!"
He somehow managed to stop Ninym from committing an act of bar-
barity and twirled the potato in his hand as he spoke. "At any rate,
getting rid of this mine isn't a matter of 'if.' The only problem is finding
the best timing to get the opportunity back."

"The entire army will fight until the bitter end to keep it, so it'll be
impossible to make them give that up without a strong incentive."

"Marden is gonna lead a huge army here. Once we face them, battle
fatigue is bound to hit our men hard, whether they like it or not."

"The strength of their army is proportionate to our ego. Won't it get
our troops fired up instead?"

"I think we'll have to fight at least one battle," Wein mumbled, dis-
satisfied. "If there's any more bloodshed, their morale will take a hit.
Besides, even now, Marden is probably hoping to settle things quickly,
even though we've failed to negotiate. If it comes to a stalemate, we can
reconcile with them and sell back the mine…!"

"You just won't give up, will you?"

"Give up? Come on! How could I? As it is, the bill is through the
roof. If there's gold for the taking, you bet I'll grab it with all I've got!"

"Okay, okay, fine. Well then, should I keep an eye on Marden's
movements and prepare for the upcoming siege?"

"Sounds like a plan." Wein nodded and continued on. "One more
thing. We've got a few informants in their royal palace, right?"

"Yes, just a small number in both the Mahdia and Stella factions."

"Well, get them to hint that the Stella might make a move and
that they might take back the mine soon. Make it seem as natural as
possible."

"I'll see to it."

"I'd also like to talk to Raklum and Pelynt about battle positions."

"Understood. I'll call them in on the way."

Ninym turned on her heel and exited the room. Left alone, Wein
distracted himself and played with the potato for a while.

He looked up at the ceiling. "Doesn't look like I can just leave the next one in Hagal's hands... Guess it's my turn now."

Ninym found Raklum near the entrance to the mine, where he was talking with Pelynt about the location and condition of the tunnels.

"Commander Raklum, His Highness wishes to see you. Pelynt, he asks that you join him."

"Certainly. I'll be there immediately."

Raklum had many duties, including giving orders to the soldiers and keeping channels of communication open with the residents. But whenever Wein called for him, he was ready to answer at the drop of a hat. The two men headed toward the building together.

"Commander Raklum, might I ask a question?" started Pelynt.

"But of course."

Raklum had recently been appointed to handle business affairs, and Pelynt acted as the head of the mine, so the two were in close contact with each other and on friendly terms. He was asking this question as a matter of course.

"Is that Flahm girl His Highness's favorite concubine or something...?"

"......"

Raklum jolted to a stop, and the air around them grew heavy. Pelynt realized he'd clearly misspoken, and his eyes went to the sword at Raklum's side. He was fully prepared to die.

"...Sir Pelynt. Come to think of it, you are from Marden, correct?"

"...Yes, I am." Pelynt nodded slowly. He'd escaped death in that moment, but he could tell it was still very close to swinging the other way.

"Then I suppose it's unsurprising you find our ways strange. After all, the Flahm aren't treated very well in the West."

"......"

"Lady Ninym is irreplaceable to His Highness. I'm sure she acts as a concubine in some aspects, but she's so much more. She is an important aide and a friend without equal."

"That is... I see. It appears I've been terribly rude."

"No, no need to apologize. I'm thankful you brought it to my attention. We're no longer in the royal palace, after all, and I keep forgetting there are many who don't know Lady Ninym." Raklum closed his eyes to gather his thoughts. "Sir Pelynt, His Highness is kindhearted and a lord worth serving—but, like all kings, he possesses an unspeakable wrath."

"......"

"As far as I know, there have been three people who've publicly insulted Lady Ninym."

"...And what happened to those people?"

"They're gone."

Pelynt quickly understood what Raklum was trying to imply.

"Sir Pelynt, I don't have the authority to give you orders, so it goes without saying that this is nothing but an appeal: See to it that both you and your subordinates watch your words."

"...I understand. But if someone's tongue does slip," he started.

"If it does..." Raklum tapped the hilt of his sword menacingly. "...it'll be better to pretend they never existed in the first place. If we wake the sleeping dragon, he could very well lose control."

"......" Pelynt didn't say another word. The two carried this silence between them until they arrived at Wein's office.

"Your Highness. It is Raklum and Pelynt."

"Come in."

They entered the room. Pelynt's face still looked nervous from their conversation earlier. They both took a knee upon seeing Wein seated in his chair.

"I have come at your request."

"I heard there is a task for me as well. Please ask of me what you will."

Wein listened to their statements and nodded. "Did you hear about our negotiations with Marden the other day?"

"Yes, such news has reached my ears."

"Well then, this should go quickly. There's no longer any chance of avoiding battle with Marden. We'll have multiple war councils from now on to hammer out the details, but we'll most likely decide to ultimately defend the mine and fight them there. So there's something I want you two to work on ahead of time." Wein grinned and began to explain his plan.

While Natra was outlining its defense strategy, Marden was moving to take back the gold mine.

"How many soldiers do we have?" In the royal court, Minister Holonyeh was spearheading battle preparations.

"We currently have around twenty thousand."

"Much less than we planned. What's going on?"

"The head of the Mahdia's Monas family is still reluctant to join the troops."

"How preposterous! At a time like this! Tell them the king will have their heads if they throw any more tantrums."

"Understood!"

He issued more orders to his subordinates, then headed for the king's hall.

As Holonyeh stood before him, King Fyshtarre made no effort to hide his irritation. "Holonyeh, why haven't you eliminated those pests yet?"

"My king, please wait just a short while longer. I promise to bring you glorious victory…"

"That much is a given! Listen, those fools were insolent enough to turn down an offer to talk this out! These gnats have forgotten their station and sullied my name for a second time! There will be hell to pay!"

Even though King Fyshtarre had zero interest in diplomacy from the very beginning, it was unacceptable for anyone to reject an offer made in his name. He considered the Kingdom of Natra to be far beneath him, and he couldn't imagine the correct response to his proposal to be anything other than humble bootlicking.

Holonyeh still couldn't stop laughing about it. Thanks to Minister Midan advocating for a diplomatic resolution, his political opponent had been cast aside by the king and his influence at least halved. On top of that, Holonyeh was trusted with commanding the upcoming battle. Meaning the Stella had all the power. No one was left to stand in his way. If he succeeded in taking back the gold mine, his position in the royal palace would be set. He'd drive out the Mahdia blight and have both the politically clueless king and the rest of the country under his thumb.

However, a pitifully small country like this will not satisfy me... I'll have to go big.

More ambitious efforts and a clear path ahead filled him with immense joy.

As he stood gloating, the voice of someone important reached his ears.

"Is this where you were, my king?"

A handsome man clad in armor appeared before Holonyeh and the king. He was the young general Draghwood, one of the Stella and a full supporter of Holonyeh.

"I apologize deeply for my tardiness. I, Draghwood, have arrived at His Royal Majesty's request."

"Hmph, about time..."

As Draghwood loudly declared his loyalty, Fyshtarre gave him a sour look and sniffed.

It was common knowledge among the retainers that Fyshtarre hated Draghwood, jealous of his good looks. Even so, now that Marden was late in the game, even Fyshtarre knew he couldn't cast him aside—especially for a reason as petty as his face.

Moreover, the general's youth and good looks were no accident. His handsome features would quickly make him popular with the people, and his youthful lack of experience meant he would be easy to keep a handle on. Draghwood was chosen to put on a good face and make a push for the Stella, more than for his talents and gifts.

"Welcome back, General Draghwood. I can only imagine the difficulties you've suffered while protecting our western lands."

"There were no major encounters; it was relatively peaceful."

It was true. Western Marden was stable, so he was really only there to gain clout. It was impossible for him to fail in such a place, however talentless he might be.

"The soldiers keeping an eye on Natra are the ones facing the heat." Draghwood was well aware of the ongoing war with Natra in the east.

"I'm going to have you command our troops in order to take back the stolen lands. You'll agree to do this, right?" Fyshtarre commanded.

"Yes, of course." He gave a smile full of confidence. "The people of Natra are a band of savages who don't know the teachings of Levetia. When I heard our beloved country had been ravaged by such people, I was ashamed and humiliated for letting this come to pass. In the name of our god and our king, let me show them where they belong."

The troops gathered into formation to take back their mine. All together, they amassed to thirty thousand soldiers. Draghwood the Stella stood at the great host's head. Their supreme commander was a symbol of their military prowess.

As the continent greeted the coming summer, both the Natra and Marden armies were set to clash in a brutal fight.

A unique feature of the Jilaat mine was that it had the mountain ridge circling in an arc around the main quarry. From overhead, it looked like the tail of a curled beast. The summit was at a relatively gentle incline, but nothing was there except rocks and sand. Ore was still

being excavated from tunnels halfway up the mountain. Hardly anyone had traveled so high up.

—Until now. The main camp of the Kingdom of Natra's army sat at
the very top of the mine.

"Well, I gotta say. This makes for one hell of a view," Wein murmured
as he stared down at the foot of the mountain from his headquarters.

Surrounding the gold mine was the full might of the Marden army,
ready and in position—easily over thirty thousand men.

"Five thousand versus thirty thousand. Hopeless, of course," he
commented.

Ninym sighed beside him. Five thousand. That was all they had to
defend themselves. Of course, they had the supplies to last through a
siege, and everything had been meticulously planned. But this large
a gap in numbers was sobering to say the least.

Even so, neither of them thought this would lead to a heroic tragedy.

"So, twenty-five thousand at the front of the mine and five thousand
in the back?" he confirmed.

"The back is basically a wall. That'd be pretty difficult to climb.
That said, it still feels like the Marden forces are being sloppy by not
stationing enough of their men below."

"Not much surprise there," he remarked knowingly. "It isn't their
main goal to annihilate our troops. In fact, if we tried to escape from
the back, they'd probably be happy about it."

Now Wein was certain that this overwhelming enemy still had
weaknesses he could take advantage of.

"Ninym, where is everyone?"

"They're ready for you."

"All right, guess we better have one last meeting before the battle."

Wein and Ninym made their way to one of the makeshift tents.

"General Draghwood, the troops are ready."

"Good work."

While Wein and Ninym had been gazing down the mountain, the

Marden army was staring up at the gold mine. Their force was thirty thousand strong, assembled by loosening Marden's purse strings and paying out a handsome sum.

This was the first time Draghwood had taken to the field with such a large army. It was a first for Marden, too. But his handsome face showed no signs of nervousness or worry, more along the lines of compassion and mercy.

"To have to face this many soldiers while holed up in a castle with no way to retreat... How foolish," he said.

"Shall I take that as a testament of their courage?"

The adjutant's reply was likely meant as a joke, but Draghwood shook his head tragically.

"This can't even be called blind courage. They fundamentally lack the common sense to understand they're as good as done. Anyone else would've been able to measure just how much of a disadvantage they're at. Honestly, if we are to fight like wild animals, I hope they at least have the animal instinct to know when to quit. Less blood to be spilled."

"As expected of you. To extend kindness and compassion to the enemy."

"You have to remember: This isn't a battle between humans. We've been ordered to exterminate vermin. I mean, that'd drive anyone to extend some kindness." Draghwood looked up. "I'll make this quick and painless. I can at least do that much."

"—Right on schedule."

When Wein sat back in his chair at the war council, those were the first words out of his mouth. Inside the tent were the commanding officers. Raklum and Hagal were present. There was no unrest among them, and everyone knew he wasn't bluffing.

"It was worth instigating events within their royal palace. There's no question the enemy is looking for a quick fight."

"They're hoping to overpower us with a large force so that we have no choice but to make our escape. If we don't, they'll take over the mine in one go. Is that right?"

"Yeah. This way, we've at least got a chance."

The worst-case scenario would be getting caught in a battle of attrition where the Natra army would be forced to use up their limited stamina. If that's what the Marden wanted to do, they would have prepared a few thousand soldiers to keep an eye on the mine and cut off Natra's trade and supplies—instead of sending a massive army.

That would've been effective, seeing the surrounding regions were still under the control of Marden, and Wein was in a semi-isolated location. It wouldn't be easy to maintain his force's strength and continue protecting the mine if they couldn't replenish their supplies. If things became dragged out, they'd be driven into a corner, and Natra would be the first to raise a white flag.

But Marden didn't do that. They were too caught up fretting about the gold mine, their nation's lifeline. They couldn't bear to have it taken away from them for another second.

"There's no question they really struggled to pull together thirty thousand soldiers. Their army will use up a ton of resources and supplies from day one, and they're sure to be short on guards along the country's borders. In that case, they won't be able to keep this up for very long. I'd say—they'll probably last about a month."

He'd come to this conclusion after compiling the information his spies had gathered. It was very accurate.

If they held out against Marden for a month and forced them to withdraw, Natra would be rewarded with renewed confidence, and Marden might realize they weren't going down so easily.

Then I might get a second chance at reconciliation...!

He wouldn't fail this time. As he carried this mistake with him, Wein announced, "Let's go, everyone—it's gonna be a messy month."

Marden made the first move. That went without saying.

There were three paths in the mountains leading up to the mine, and the Marden soldiers rushed up each of them simultaneously. Of course, Natra's forces were waiting for them at each path, and the sharp sound of battle echoed through the region.

"Forward! Crawl over your dead comrades if you have to! Keep moving!"

"Stop them! Kick them off the path!"

On either side, the angry roars of soldiers and barked commands flew in every direction. The battlefield was submerged in heat and passion. But it was only the beginning. The determination to win rose to the surface on both sides.

"Oh, looks like Natra's got some spirit after all."

"Ha-ha-ha, a brush with death will make anyone frantic."

"Seeing how long they can keep up should be fun."

In an unexpected turn of events, the Marden commanders found that their enemy wouldn't go down easily at the start of the battle. But as they observed their opponents, they remained perfectly calm. The enemy's strength was only temporary. Besides, their own military force made it obvious there was no cause for concern.

In less than a few hours, we should be able to take the mountain's third station...

Back at the royal palace, Draghwood had made the firm promise that Natra would fall within the week. At this rate, it'd likely be less than half that time. As he thought of their triumphant return in the near future, he broke into a small smile. Then, just as expected, his soldiers began to grow adjusted to the battle. A change in tides burst forth.

However, it sorely went awry.

"...What's this?"

The Marden forces were being pushed back.

"What's going on...?"

Peeking down the edge of the mountain summit, Pelynt was bewildered when he saw the scene below.

Since this was war and the residents of the mine were civilians, many of them fled to Natra. Those who chose to remain were conscripted as soldiers. Even so, they had hardly any training and primarily worked as military engineers.

Pelynt had stayed behind to continue acting as a mediator and now stood in the middle of a war zone. His heart swirled with feelings of anxiety and doubt. The enemy had thirty thousand soldiers. Thirty thousand. Upon hearing these numbers, Pelynt prepared for death. Being back under Marden's rule would leave him with no more than a few years anyway. *Falling on the battlefield to repay His Highness wouldn't be so bad*: That had been his line of thinking when he chose to stay.

"Why do we have the upper hand...?" he wondered aloud.

The state of the battle was beyond his expectations. One after the other, the soldiers of Natra rotated between repelling the Marden men on the mountain path and blocking their way.

As he stared down in confusion, he heard a voice behind him. "There are a number of reasons."

Startled, Pelynt quickly turned around in surprise. "Y-Your Highness?!"

"Relax. As you were." Wein held out a hand to stop Pelynt from taking a knee as he walked over to stand by his side.

"First of all, their men must have trained separately. Look at the back of the Marden army. There's kind of a whitish group there, right?"

"Y-yes. That is...?"

"Their commander Draghwood's elite forces. They look white from the light reflecting off their armor. Now, what about the Marden soldiers at the foot of the mountain?"

"...They aren't very well equipped."

"Exactly." He nodded. "Most of their army consists of farmers, paid to fight. Draghwood is too stingy to use his elites and tossed the untrained soldiers into battle first. But our troops were trained to the Empire's standards, plus we have pride and confidence from beating them last time. We're no pushovers," he scoffed. "On top of that—at this time of year, there is a strong air current that blows from the summit to the foot of the mountain. Thanks to that, our arrows can catch the wind and reach deep into the heart of the enemy. On the flip side, their arrows drop halfway. We've also placed guards in blind spots and set up a number of trenches to weaken the enemy's offense—but most important is this terrain we're fighting on."

"The terrain?"

"Five thousand versus thirty thousand. The numbers are scary at a glance, but take a look. How many do you think are fighting right now?"

Upon hearing this, a realization struck Pelynt. There were thirty thousand enemy soldiers, but in reality, the vast majority were idly circling around them—doing nothing in particular. Only a few hundred were actually fighting.

"The mountain paths aren't wide by any means. There's no way for them to fully deploy thousands of soldiers. As a result, it went from five thousand versus thirty thousand to a few hundred from each side each duking it out. Doesn't that just tickle you, Pelynt? The rest of them are simply a bunch of freeloaders, getting meals for no work in return."

"I see… So that's why you suddenly had the miners shave down the mountain. It was to create a greater incline to stop the Marden from advancing in large numbers, I'm guessing?"

"Exactly. It's not so bad if you're agile and not loaded down by a weapon, but trying to ascend a slope with swords and spears is hell. Even if you claw your way up, our soldiers are waiting for you at the top. They've got no choice but to use the designated roads."

"However, with all due respect, what if the Marden forge their own path…?"

"We won't have to worry about that for a while," Wein said, shaking his head. "They probably would have considered making new paths if there weren't any roads at all, or if they were narrower and fewer in number. But there are three to choose from, and it's not impossible to fight on them. Carving their own way would take time and require the right tools." Wein gave a smirk. "They're not willing to spare the extra labor. It's easier to use the paths as they are—and they *love* things that are easy. At this point, they think they can depend on brute force. My plan is all about making them believe that."

"……" At last, Pelynt understood.

Unless this boy was just plain nice, he didn't enter a battle to die an honorable death for his people. In the back of Wein's mind, there was a world only he could see, and he knew for certain there was a path to victory.

"Well, we can chat more later. How's the other matter coming along, Pelynt?"

"Ah… Yes, sir! The construction is complete and ready to go at any time."

"Good work."

Wein's eyes fixated on a single point. Marden's headquarters. Their commander, Draghwood, was probably there.

"These little surprises should be making him pull at his hair right about now, but…I'll have him around my pinkie for a little while longer."

"—How is such idiocy even possible?!"

Draghwood's angry voice echoed inside the tent. The other commanders hung their heads and kept silent. As if trying to escape from the brunt of his rage, they all put on as stoic a face as they could muster.

"It's thirty thousand against five thousand…! How are you failing to take control of one mountain?!"

Three days had passed since the start of the battle. And Marden had achieved absolutely nothing in that time.

Their investigations showed the Kingdom of Natra's army had placed their main guard at the first, second, and third stations: the critical junctures. On top of that, they had a large store of supplies stashed inside the mine and a system that allowed the front line to be replenished through a series of checkpoints so they could continue to fight.

This was also a difficult battlefield: Trenches had been built in front of each juncture, and the extra dirt had been used to form a steep wall. Not to mention the soldiers on patrol were the physical manifestations of power and might. They cleverly worked together to fend off the Marden soldiers trying to climb up and quickly replaced the fatigued and injured with backup.

Marden's lack of preparation showed. In a sense, the Natra army had transformed the entire mountain into a fortress, while his men had sauntered onto the battlefield with equipment good for fighting on level ground—not storming castles.

They, of course, checked for new paths and gaps in their opponent's defense strategy, but none of the results led to anything. They were stuck in this predicament. Even their extensive resources were continuing to dwindle, and the prolonged, fruitless assault was taking a toll on the soldiers' morale.

"These damn savage barbarians...!" Draghwood's resentment refused to cool down. Lesser life-forms had gotten the jump on him and led him around by the nose. He covered his bruised pride with outward rage.

A messenger came flying into the tent.

"My apologies!"

"What is it?!" Draghwood barked. "Can't you see we're in the middle of a war council?"

Faced with a death glare, the messenger shook as he spoke. "D-deepest apologies. I have an important report from the soldiers who scouted the area..."

"Well?"

"Sir... The truth is, they've discovered old tunnels possibly leading inside the mine."

"What?!"

A small commotion rippled among the commanders.

"I need details. Where is it?!"

"Hey, bring a map of the area around the mine!"

They hurriedly spread the map inside the tent. The gold mine was in the center, and the mountain ridge circled around it. The messenger pointed.

"They discovered tunnels near this part of the ridge, and when they investigated the inside, it seemed clearly man-made."

"You mean the cave itself is natural?"

"Yes, but take it with a grain of salt: It's a report from some soldiers. But based on their findings, they wonder if those who dug it gave up upon reaching the cave."

"Have they confirmed where it leads to?"

"It's appears to be long, but there's been no confirmation yet. They wished to confer with you first."

The messenger finished his report, and the commanders looked at one another. Amid their predicament, they'd found a new path that led them straight to the heart of their enemy. Each of them knew they were at a vital crossroad and needed to approach their next move with caution.

"General Draghwood, let's investigate as soon as possible. If the tunnels lead inside the mine, we can instantly change the course of this war."

"I'd hate to waste time by working on something as tedious as an investigation. Let's send in two thousand men? Fortunately—eh, that might not be the right word—we have plenty of soldiers waiting on standby. If it's a false flag, we can easily call them back."

"Won't that tip them off? I mean, we might finally have the chance to launch a surprise attack," suggested another officer.

The commanders continued to trade opinions and strategies while Draghwood listened on in silence.

"—All right," he finally muttered. "I know what to do."

It'd been a week since they started to fight.

General fatigue hung over the battlefield. The Marden men were unable to break through the defenses, and the soldiers of Natra were unable to leave their fortified mine. With hand-to-hand combat peaking on day three, the standstill was quickly becoming a glaring contest.

This day ended with nothing more than sporadic clashes close to the paths. Both armies started setting up camp and went to sleep while a few kept watch.

Late into the night, there was some movement at the cave, surrounded by the trees and out of plain sight. Coupled with thick clouds veiling the moon, the night was dark and ominous. The inside of the cave was as black as if the darkness had been brewed and boiled, and it spewed forth an inky mess. An ebony silhouette oozed out of its entrance.

Not just one. Two, three, more, soundlessly followed. Then, in the blink of an eye, the number swelled to dozens more—

"—Light the torches!"

The cave flooded with light, illuminating a wide-eyed group of a few dozen Natra keeping watch, and over a hundred Marden soldiers carrying their burning lights in formation.

"It's a trap! Retreat!" yelled a person in the smaller group.

"After them! Don't let a single one get away!" shouted the impenetrable lineup as the two groups started to move simultaneously in an elaborate theater of hunter and prey.

It's just as General Draghwood predicted!

Joining in on this dramatic chase was the commander in charge, Anglyru, smiling in satisfaction.

On the third day of the battle, Draghwood, upon finding out about the tunnels, had said: "First of all, we don't know whether the tunnels actually lead anywhere useful inside of the mine. But if it does, there's no way Natra wouldn't know about it, right?"

"...You're completely right."

Of course, Natra would have investigated the inside of the gold mine the moment they got their hands on it, seeing they also had access to the miners and their knowledge. In fact, it would've been odd for them *not* to notice it.

"In that case, Natra has two ways to deal with this: either destroy it to prevent any outside forces from infiltrating into their main base or use it. My guess is the latter."

"Why?"

"Well, you see, the tunnels can be used as an emergency escape route and to send out soldiers to launch a surprise attack. Once they realize we've found their tunnels, they might try to bury them, but if they're oblivious, it'll give us an ace up our sleeve."

"How should we carry this out? Should we send soldiers and rush in after all?"

"No. It would be better to trap these beasts," Draghwood spat, giving a twisted smile.

Truth be told, he was deeply humiliated by these barbarians and their effective counterattack. By trapping the Natra soldiers, he knew he'd heal his wounded pride.

In fact, the other commanders more or less wanted to move forward with this plan, too, so nobody pointed out that he wasn't exactly thinking clearly.

"For now, we'll keep the battle going and force them into a deadlock."

"A-are you sure, sir?"

"It's fine. If we enter a standstill, those lowlifes will see their chance and stir up trouble. And if the tunnels really do connect to the inside, there's a good chance they'll use the cave to do so... Anglyru!"

"Yes, sir!" Anglyru promptly bowed.

"You are to lead five hundred men to the perimeter of the cave and lie in wait. Starting now! When those guys come crawling out of the cave, kill 'em and storm in to finish the job," he ordered. "They might be at an advantage now since they're using the mountain paths to push us back. But they pose no threat on level ground. Plus, they're such a small army that losing even a few dozen men is a fatal blow."

"Please leave it to me! I shall smoke out those pathetic dogs and lay them to waste!"

These orders were the reason why Anglyru had hidden outside the cave. Four nights had passed, and now he was chasing after the fleeing lot, all according to plan.

"Go! Go! Don't let 'em escape!" he barked as he ran through the dim cave, torch in one hand.

At the very least, he knew the tunnels were connected to the gold mine. That much was certain. When they reached the center, he and his men would rush in and tear the enemy army apart, and the first victory of the battle would be his.

They sure were quick to run, he thought in scorn and admiration.

As soon as they'd crawled out of the cave, he'd thought he had caught them completely off guard. But they'd turned tail almost immediately and scampered into the cave without a single casualty.

Beasts. The right thing to do is designate a few soldiers to buy enough time for someone to warn others of danger ahead. But I suppose fleeing for your own dear life is nature's instinct when it comes down to these animals.

Their enemy's speed was just as animalistic. Even though there was hardly enough light to see anything, they darted deeper and deeper into the cave without stumbling once.

—Hmph. That's…

Before Anglyru's eyes was a tunnel at the back of the jet-black cave, its periphery illuminated by bonfires. He caught the Natra soldiers scuttling inside the rocky path.

"They went down that way! After them!" Anglyru blared, slightly out of breath.

Not that his physical condition was something worth noting. After all, he was running at full speed in armor and carrying a sword, and around him, soldiers started to have the same trouble.

…Huh? he thought with a start, upon reaching the entrance to the tunnel. *What about the enemy?*

Of course, Anglyru and his soldiers were fully equipped. Why wouldn't they be? They'd come to fight. But what about Natra?

...Nothing. They have nothing on them.

The Marden chased them into the tunnel. After all, those were the orders. It was why they came. *Hold up. Wait. Something is off.* As they hastened after them, an alarm rang inside his head.

Their enemy had no weapons or armor, and though they should've been caught off guard, they had made a splendid escape. On top of it all, they were visible during the entire chase even though they should've been able to quickly outpace the Marden forces due to being dozens of pounds lighter.

No, it can't be.

They continued the chase, and he looked back. About ten soldiers followed behind. It was an exceedingly narrow tunnel. It was too late to either stop or turn around.

Have I just been lured into a—?

In the next moment, a thunderous, clamorous bang rang in his head, and Anglyru's consciousness fell into darkness.

"—You're telling me they failed?"

The messenger's report drained all color from Draghwood's face.

"Yes… They followed orders to wait outside the cave. When a few dozen Natra soldiers emerged from it, they followed Captain Anglyru's command to pursue the fleeing lot into the inner tunnels, but…"

"But what? Spit it out!"

"…it collapsed. The tunnel fell down on them: Captain Anglyru and a hundred others were crushed on impact."

"……" Draghwood's lips trembled. The wooden bowl in his hand burst into a million pieces. "YOU SWINE—PIGS, BEASTS, DAMN STUPID IDIOTS!"

Unable to contain his rage any longer, he punted the chair and bashed it with his fists. "HOW DARE THOSE MANGY, HEA-THEN DOGS TRY TO MAKE A FOOL OUT OF ME…!"

"G-General, please try to calm down."

"Y-yes," placated a commander. "We understand losing Anglyru is big. But we lost only a hundred soldiers. No more than a hundred men out of thousands."

He had a valid point. Even with all the dead and injured since the start of the war, they still had plenty of soldiers—over twenty thousand. One hundred men wouldn't make much of a difference.

"Those Natra are no doubt throwing themselves a victory banquet, but this supposed 'win' is nothing more than a misunderstanding. *We* are the true winners: Our men closed off their escape route."

Hearing them prattle on and on helped Draghwood finally regain his composure. He released a big sigh and picked up the fallen chair.

"…You know what? You're right. One hundred people. It's only one hundred," Draghwood said to himself as he turned to the messenger. "Is it possible to fix the cave-in?"

"According to the reports, it'd take around one or two months."

"It might as well be a dead end in this battle…" the general brusquely concluded, looking out above the tents and glaring at the summit beyond them. "Enjoy yourselves, savages. This small wound had no effect on us…!"

"—To be honest, it effects them a lot." Wein was coincidentally laughing in a tent at the top of the mountain.

"Really? Even though we took out only a hundred of thirty thousand?" Ninym questioned.

The two were alone, so they didn't bother mincing words.

"You're right that we barely managed to damage their troops. We lured them in as far as we could to trap them, but the tunnel was super-narrow. Even though the miners did an awesome job setting off the trap, we can't expect too much more. But our target wasn't the soldiers."

She tilted her head. "Then who?"

He lightly tapped his chest with his thumb. "The hearts of the leaders controlling the army. That's what I was trying to get at."

In a start, she remembered something. "That's why you had me research their supreme commander in such detail."

"Yep. Long story short, Draghwood is a member of the Stella elite and a devoted follower of the teachings of Levetia, which basically means he sees us as a ragtag group of barbarians."

"...Well, he must've been under a lot of stress, seeing he couldn't make any progress in this battle fighting against us 'savages.'"

"That's when the information about tunnels was floated toward him like a lifeboat. A chance at recovery. But Draghwood got greedy, unsatisfied with simply sending in soldiers. He just had to lay a trap and chase us to prove he was better than some beasts."

"And suffered even more humiliation as a result."

"Exactly." Wein looked at the map, where there was a neat line of pawns symbolizing the enemy. There were significantly fewer pieces around the mine. "I have no way of defeating an army of thirty thousand with only five thousand," he admitted. "But I *can* go for the commanders behind them."

His fingers gripped around the innermost piece, the enemy's headquarters.

"When the heart suffers fresh wounds, it can hinder the decision-making process. The more we injure Draghwood, the duller their army's movements will become. He's stumbling along just the way we hoped he would."

Watching her master fiddle with a pawn, Ninym shrugged. "I've always thought this, Wein, but you really do have an awful personality."

He smirked. "I'll take that as a compliment."

"Charge! Go forward!"

"Today's the day we take down their filthy base!"

"YEAAAAAAAAAH!"

©Falmaro

The Marden forces took their aggression one step further, attacking their enemy with more fervor than before, as if to compensate for their losses.

Their strategy was to continue applying pressure in numbers—simple, but difficult to fight against. Even the Natra soldiers were starting to feel the losses after beating back their enemy time and time again, only to be met with more soldiers.

As the days progressed, the Natra forces destroyed their own positions near the first station on the mountain paths, as if to say they couldn't take it anymore. They then pulled their lines farther up the hill.

Hearing this report made Draghwood's perpetual frown break into a smile, and the Marden soldiers finally felt as if they were making headway. Relief spread across the army.

—But this moment didn't escape Wein's attention.

"Raklum."

"Sir."

Under the moonlight, Wein and Raklum stood alongside each other on the summit. Below them was the sleeping Marden army. A night watch was on guard, but it was easy to tell they were being careless. It was understandable. The Marden found strength in numbers, and though their men had attacked at night, there had been no retaliation from Natra so far. On top of that, they'd just gained the upper hand tonight, putting them in a good mood. An army consisting mostly of farmers couldn't help but let their guard down.

For this reason, Wein told Raklum, "Be flashy, but don't play around like you did in the Polta Wasteland."

"Leave it to me." Raklum gave a solid nod as he jumped on his horse.

The horses had been brought to the summit beforehand, and about thirty cavalrymen were majestically waiting behind Raklum, ready to set out.

"Well, let's get started—all units, move out!"

At his order, the thirty horses simultaneously galloped down the steep mountain into the night.

The cavalrymen darted down the mountain on horseback, setting ablaze as many enemy tents as they could, continuously moving from one location to another so as not to get caught.

Those were the only orders Wein had given Raklum's group. But they had gotten in-depth information about their enemy in order to carry this out.

"Right now, I'm going to tell you what I've observed from the enemy's movements this week."

Wein had talked about the sleeping quarters of the low-level units—those structures were their targets. He had discussed at length how to spread fire according to predicted wind directions. He had designated soldiers for this attack, their route to take to advance, and possible escape routes.

Watching him spread the map, place the pawns, and speak in minute detail, Raklum had been unable to hide his admiration.

It was information anyone could have gathered if they had taken the time to investigate the Marden army. But how many people could actually pull off such a thing?

On top of this plan, Wein had made them practice traveling down the mountain on horseback before the war. He'd been drawing this plan in his head ever since.

"That's the plan. Any questions?"

Of course, there hadn't been any.

What they *did* have was confidence this plan would work.

—And here they were.

The thirty cavalrymen galloped past the confusion and chaos spreading among the Marden as the flames started to engulf them.

"What the hell's going on?!" "Wake everyone up to help put out the flames! It's spreading!" "It's the cavalry! I saw them start the fire!" "Where are they?! Where'd they go?!"

Frantic roars and screams leaped out of their mouths. But nothing more happened. By the time the Marden forces recovered from their state of shock and took up their bows and swords, their enemy was already long gone, kicking up dust in their wake.

"They really fell for it, huh, Captain? Almost makes you feel bad for laughing!"

Raklum listened to the excited voices clamor behind him. There was no doubt it'd been a success. The unit had rushed down the mountain before the snoozing soldiers had a chance to respond. No one had been able to stop them from spreading the fire.

"Ha-ha! Just look at those Marden fools. They're runnin' around all over without even any weapons."

"Their stupidity is a blessing. Thanks to that, we were able to fly right through."

With a job well done, the soldier's faces relaxed. But unlike the others, Raklum was tense. If the Marden army was an ocean, his team of cavalrymen created a high tide, thanks to Wein's keen knowledge of its coastal conditions. But as his men continued onward, he worried they might alter the current and create a whole new series of large, crashing waves.

To a sea of thirty thousand, a group of thirty soldiers was nothing more than a pebble. If they misread the direction of the current, the small Natra detachment faced the possibility of being crushed to dust in an instant.

But that was why Wein had chosen Raklum as captain.

"—Left face!" he yelled, and the cavalry simultaneously made a hard turn.

As they shifted their gaze to the hill in front of them, they realized that the initial chaos had subsided and that over a hundred Marden soldiers were pulling themselves together and gathering into formation.

If the men on horseback had just plunged right on in, their movements would've been halted.

"That's our commander Raklum for you. That's one sharp nose."

"I refuse to ruin His Highness's plan with carelessness," he replied coolly. "...It's almost time," he breathed out as a strange rumbling reached the ground beneath them.

"All right! All units, escape formation!"

The horses had their physical limits. After exerting all their energy to wreak havoc on the Marden, the cavalry had to get out of there before it became impossible for the horses to move altogether. This thundering noise was their cue. Well, to be exact, it was more than just a signal. It was another plan being carried out, not at all related to Raklum's group.

"Don't get out of formation! We've got to make it to the foot of the mountain in one go!"

"Roger that!"

Raklum and his men synchronously turned their reins toward the mine.

Sensing a commotion, Draghwood sprang up from his nap, hastily grabbed his sword propped up nearby, and dashed out of the tent. Before his eyes were a number of fires flaring up around the foot of the mountain.

"General! It's an enemy attack!" The adjutant ran up to Draghwood, who was standing there wide-eyed. "Just now, we've gotten reports that their cavalry came down from the mountain and ran around setting fire to our encampment!"

"What?!"

Going down the mountain slopes—cliffs—by horse at night was insanity. But they must have managed to do it, seeing that the place was now surrounded by flames.

"How many?!"

"I-I'm not sure! It's complicated: Some are saying less than a hundred, while others are saying hundreds!"

The Natra couldn't have possibly hidden hundreds of horses in the mine. Maybe one hundred at most. Draghwood came to this conclusion swiftly on his own and moved on to the next question.

"Where are they now?!"

"That's unknown as well! It seems with all these fires and ensuing chaos, some of our men have not only helped out our enemy but also taken their side!"

"Ggh...!"

Their enemy was clever—much too clever. He had to put a stop to the madness first, but where to even start? Hesitation flitted inside Draghwood's mind. As if to mock him, another situation suddenly cropped up.

"—Wh-what?!"

A noise. A loud sound.

Even amid the tumultuous scene, the strange nose reached his men's ears. It sounded like the rumble of a large mass coming down from the mine.

It couldn't be, Draghwood told himself. *Their entire army is coming down the mountain all at once...?!*

Their opponent's plan was to send in the cavalry first to stir up trouble, then use the main force to finish off the confused soldiers. Shaking his head furiously, Draghwood saw the situation to come.

Absolutely idiotic! We may be confused, but there's thirty thousand of us! We can't be beaten by a mere five thousand men!

But the truth was, it *was* the sound of a large army descending upon them. They must have a target. Something valuable enough to warrant the attention of five thousand soldiers. That was— *The headquarters?! Here?!*

If it was impossible to fight the Marden military head-on, what if Natra narrowed their target down to this one area? What if their plan was to take the Marden army off guard and run right through them—to take the commanders' heads?

It's...plausible!

Of course, everything Draghwood had thought of was only conjecture. But there was no time to ponder it further.

"Gather all the surrounding troops here and take the defensive!" he barked. "Have any far-off camps do the same and prepare to stand by! Gathering our forces takes priority! Even if they spot an enemy force!"

"Y-yes, sir!" As the adjutant quickly relayed this to the messengers, they scattered in every which way.

As Draghwood continued to order the nearby men, he sharply glared at the mine. "Barbaric savages, don't you dare underestimate me. You won't take my head so easily…!"

From then on, the Marden army moved swiftly, carrying out their commander's orders. Their headquarters was reinforced with a defense team, prepared to lie in wait for their opponent. By that time, the harrowing rumbling had already stopped. What could their enemy be doing? Were they unsure of what to do next? Or secretly making their move?

It wasn't an option to piece together the entire story in the dead of night. Tension among the soldiers only continued to rise. However, when the skies finally began to clear, a new development smacked Draghwood right in the face.

"No way…!"

The Natra army hadn't come down from the mountain.

What *had* come down from the mountain were huge boulders and logs. By dragging them up the summit beforehand and pushing them back down, Natra had created the illusion of a large army moving through the cliffs toward them.

Why did they do such a thing?

The answer was to secure the defensive base on the mountain path by the first station. The Marden had gone to such great pains to get it, but now Natra held it once again.

…To get ready for the enemy's attack, I fortified our headquarters and ordered any place that wouldn't reach here in time to defend themselves

independently. However, as a result, they each became isolated and couldn't collaborate with nearby groups…!

That'd been their opponent's strategy all along: isolate the soldiers stationed by the mountain paths as individual positions that only fought on their own. While headquarters was frantically upping its defenses, Natra slipped in to steal back these areas, which was their ultimate goal.

"Those damn…!"

The Marden soldiers knew how important those checkpoints were and how difficult it had been to obtain them. This loss would have a tremendous effect. After staying up all night to keep watch and breathing a sigh of relief just before dawn, this unexpected turn was going to drop their morale whether he liked it or not.

On top of that, this fire was going to cost them in damages moving forward. The situation caused so much bewilderment that the Marden started to attack their own kind. If he added up all the dead and injured during the course of this battle, it'd easily reach into the thousands. A significant amount of resources and supplies were incinerated into ashes.

It was scores worse than the cave-in. They'd fallen for a trap—again.

"DAMN THEM ALLLLLLL!" Draghwood howled into the night, unleashing his rage and resentment.

Without his knowledge, he'd found himself wrapped around their enemy's finger.

They realized they'd been fighting for half a month.

Their night raid had left Marden with seven hundred men dead and two thousand soldiers wounded. Desertion continued to be a problem, which dropped their total count to about twenty-three thousand.

Of course, it wasn't as if Natra had suffered no casualties. Out of their five thousand soldiers, three thousand were left. As a whole, their defenses were spread thin. But based on results alone, it was clear they were putting up a stiff resistance. Their soldiers understood this, and their spirits were high amid the trials they endured.

That was the most significant difference between Marden and Natra.

As his army rejoiced, Wein was in a tent locked in a staring contest with his paperwork.

"Food supplies are fine. As for other supplies…we're definitely running short, but we can still make it work."

From every direction, the reports flew in, and they were in better condition than Wein had expected.

"Man, it's so hard being right all the time! It's so *freakin'* hard when things work out exactly as planned!" he boasted sarcastically.

By his side, Ninym was in total agreement for once. "It's wonderful everything is going well. Compared with us, our enemy's offensive strength has been a lot weaker recently. Do you still think they're going to withdraw?"

Wein shook his head. "Absolutely not. There's no way. Maybe if they'd done it within a week at the very start of battle, but it's too late for them to back out now. We've given those guys a hell of a beating, and they still got nothing to show for it. They're pretty much bursting at the seams, ready to get back at us."

Wein gave a good-natured smile that said *And it's all thanks to me.*

He continued. "They must've finally realized bulldozing their way through won't work. They're probably busy concocting a new plan. I bet they'll strike back as soon as they're ready."

"By 'new plan' you mean…a siege weapon?"

"Yeah, I mean, they've only got weapons to battle on level ground. Don't you think they're scraping together a ladder or a catapult right about now?"

"Even if they brought a catapult to a mountain, they wouldn't be able to use it," she observed.

"People tend to forget the obvious when they're driven into a corner."

If his troops were able to get past Marden's next scheme, they would finally put this fighting to rest by hitting their enemy with more snags and roadblocks. With that, Marden might even start entertaining the idea of reconciling with him. Whether the crux of it survived or not was all in the groundwork.

"My plan is perfectly sane. In two weeks, we can kiss this cooped-up life good-bye."

Ninym responded with on-the-fence skepticism. "That'd be wonderful news. I've had enough of this mountain view."

"You're tellin' me. I want to kick back in the royal palace again."

"I could use a nice bath. I have to conserve hot water here."

In wartime, water was a precious commodity, doubly so when you're barricaded in your own fort. The most you could hope for was an occasional wipe down; soaking in a bathtub of hot water was out of the question.

Ninym was no exception to this rule.

"Ah, I thought you were standing so far away from me lately. Could it be because you smellOWW?!"

She'd flicked a pawn straight at Wein's cheek.

"Will you stop saying such things?"

"GWAAAAH… D-don't think this means you win."

"It's not about whether you win or lose."

As they bantered back and forth, they sensed someone entering the tent.

"Pardon me, Your Highness."

It was Raklum. Wein and Ninym righted themselves and faced him.

"What's wrong? What happened?"

"Sir. We have a messenger from Marden."

"A messenger?" He frowned.

Sending a messenger here meant Marden was hoping to negotiate a deal. It was something he'd secretly been hoping for. He should have gladly welcomed it with open arms.

But the timing was slightly off. Marden was conserving their power for a full-on assault. For them, the idea of reconciling was a mere afterthought.

Maybe we drove Marden into a corner earlier than I thought... No, that's not it. It could be they're here to throw us off before they attack. Or...

He erred on the side of caution and gave his orders. "Understood. At any rate, let's agree to meet. Ninym, hurry and set up the location. It should be...let's say about halfway up the mine. Raklum, have the guards in the area heighten security. Marden might move out while I'm still getting everything ready."

"Understood," she replied.

"Please leave it to me!"

Ninym and Raklum swiftly exited the tent. Wein used this time to continue his thoughts.

...Their homeland could have put them on hold. The Marden army is way off schedule, after all. Fyshtarre and the royal palace must be furious, wondering why they haven't gotten the mine back yet. The vassals are probably starting to sweat a little beneath the collar, too. One of 'em probably suggested this, even though it's late in the game.

And if the vassal was so important that Draghwood couldn't ignore him, he needed to at least send a messenger, even if it was just for show.

Of course, this was just Wein's hypothesis. He had no idea whether that was actually the case. But with Marden fighting past their proposed schedule, the royal court was, no doubt, pressuring them to wrap things up.

"Out of the frying pan and into the fire, huh, Draghwood?" purred Wein, picturing his opponent's dour expression in his mind.

Long story short, Wein's guess was right on the mark.

"General, another messenger from the royal palace," announced a commander.

Draghwood clicked his tongue and turned toward one of his grim-faced officers. "Handle it and get them out of here. I don't have time to deal with them right now."

"But, General, with all due respect, if we reject another messenger, they may start to wonder if something is going on…"

"They may even bring up the siege weapons we've been collecting."

"Tch…" Draghwood gritted his teeth, making no effort to hide his impatience.

This was the difference between him and Wein. The crown prince was the kingdom's new leader. Even if he didn't deliver what he promised, all he had to do was a little arm-twisting—and he had the power to see that through.

On the other hand, Draghwood was just a military commander. He could never compare to the authority of a king, who could cut off one's professional and corporeal head whenever he fancied. Draghwood needed to continue offering results—*obvious* results—to the king and his chief vassals to prevent them from offing his head.

But he couldn't do it. The mine should have been recovered in a week, but twice the time had already passed. Progress was so slow that they ended up having to request the siege weapon, a new plan. Of course, the palace would send messengers to ask what's going on. The headquarters had been able to dodge the issue and chase the messengers away so far, but time was running out. It felt as if he could hear the voice of Minister Holonyeh taking the fall for him. The minister held a shield at Draghwood's back, but even that continued to crumble away.

"…What was the message?" he asked quietly, drawing a long breath.

"Sir. We are to seize the mine immediately. To do that…we are to reach an agreement with Natra."

It was the other commanders' turns to lose their tempers.

"Absolutely moronic! A compromise—*now*?!"

"Impossible! We've spilled so much blood fighting for them! And for what?"

"General Draghwood, let's forget the gossipmongers in the royal court and move forward with the assault!"

One by one, the officers rejected this decision unanimously. But it wasn't just hubris that stood in the way of ending the war: It was also their impatience. They hadn't even received any battle honors yet.

At this stage, they couldn't possibly hope for this new plan to earn them any awards.

"......" Draghwood shared their sentiments, of course, but had to react appropriately. "Fine, send a messenger to Natra."

"G-General?!"

"But that's...!"

"Relax. It's superficial. We can send a messenger and still save face when Natra refuses our offer. In the meantime, we'll move forward and take back the mine with force. See? Everything works out."

The plan seemed to satisfy his officers, and they nodded as one.

"Logan, you go as messenger."

The man Draghwood pointed out was his adjutant. Only one of his trusted personnel could ensure all hopes of reconciliation were dashed.

"Don't kiss their ass too much," he warned. "Make them want to fight till their dying breath."

"In the end, barbarians need very little provocation, right?" Logan snarked.

"Right. But don't screw up and piss 'em off so much they kill you."

"Understood."

After reviewing the conditions of this proposal for a few hours, their messenger was sent off to the mine.

When Ninym saw the messenger arrive at the meeting, her very first thought was *This guy has no intention of negotiating* anything.

Logan spoke with arrogance, even though the man sitting on the other side of the table was a crown prince.

"For these discussions, consider my words to be those of Supreme Commander Draghwood. That said, Prince Wein, your pet dogs down here are quite well trained. General Draghwood has high regard for them."

At this, a jolt ran through the guards, surging in their bodies. If Wein hadn't held them back, Logan would've been skewered on the spot.

"Well, Sir Logan, what has brought you here to us today? Surely you wouldn't climb a mountain simply to provoke us?"

"Of course," he snorted. "We don't waste time in such useless pursuits. I've come here with one purpose: to seek reconciliation," he said, but the conditions he tossed out were absolutely absurd.

The demands included: immediate withdrawal from the mine, confiscation of all weapons, return of the mine residents, and compensation for suddenly seizing Marden territory. Wein wouldn't want to go forward with this negotiation.

"What do you think, Prince Wein?"

"Unfortunately, we cannot accept under those conditions."

It was an obvious conclusion.

"Our aim is to reach as equal a compromise as possible," claimed Logan. "However, if you prolong this war, I'm afraid your head may return to your homeland severed from your body."

"A frightening thought indeed. However, Sir Logan, I expect I'll be home returning in triumph."

"I see. It seems you're surrounded by nothing but dogs. I'm warning you only out of concern for your welfare, but you'd do well to keep company with those who question your own folly." Logan stood. It seemed the meeting would end the same way it started.

Honestly. What a waste of time. Sighing inside, Ninym already began mapping out the postmeeting cleanup in her mind.

But something unexpected stopped her in her tracks.

Logan had halted and pivoted around when Ninym caught his eye.

"You ought to toss away the ashy slave. Keeping such a filthy thing nearby is unfitting for one of noble blood," he spat.

"_____"

Logan was oblivious to the fact that the air in the room froze over.

Ninym tried to talk to Wein, but any words she wanted to say held fast in her throat. From behind, she felt an unfamiliar, bloodcurdling energy ooze out of Wein's body.

"Sir Logan." Wein's flat voice echoed in the room. "You said before that your words were those of General Draghwood... Are you sure of that?"

"They certainly are. What of it?"

"Oh, it's nothing. Please tell the general that I hope he looks after his health."

With a questioning look, Logan departed without another word.

Even after he was long gone, Wein sat motionless. As tension filled and congealed in the room, Ninym steeled herself.

"Y-Your Highness," she called out.

"I let you down, Ninym," he interrupted. "Jiva was different, so I got careless. Prejudice against the Flahm really does run deep in the West. I wasn't thinking about it clearly enough when I brought you here: I put you through a lot of pain."

"N-not at all! You did nothing of the sort..."

"I'll be more aware from now on. Well, I'll leave the rest here to you. I'll head back to headquarters."

"...Yes, understood."

Wein stood and began heading toward the summit. With his order to tidy up, Ninym could only watch his back fade into the distance.

When he was finally out of earshot, Wein growled at his guards. "Call Raklum."

A few days after this meeting, Marden was finally prepared to launch their attack. With the gold mine as its stage, the war between Marden and Natra had reached its final act.

"General, all troops are in position!"

"The ladders have been set in all directions."

"We await your order, General."

The commanders lined up in front of Draghwood were jabbering, talking on top of one another. He let out a deep sigh and gave them a piercing glare.

"It's been three weeks since the battle started. We've wasted enough time."

What was supposed to be a quick war turned into a tangled mess. Draghwood had lost his men to dirty, wicked schemes, and his once-plentiful supplies continued to edge dangerously close to rock bottom.

"This is all because of my immorality. I've caused you and everyone else great hardship."

An easy victory had been dragged on and on. He was unlikely to receive any recognition or awards for his efforts. In fact, there was more than enough possibility that he might be tried as a war criminal or something.

But none of that mattered anymore. If he could defeat the barbarians, he'd be satisfied.

"Our humiliation ends today. By the time evening comes, we'll dye this mountain red with the blood of the foreign scourge—go forth!"

""Yes, sir!""

With the sun blazing at its zenith and their sights set on the mine, the Marden were ready to launch its full-scale attack.

Soon enough, Wein caught wind of the news at the summit.

"So they're finally going for it, huh?" he mumbled to himself. He quickly issued orders to the messenger. "We're deserting the defensive posts in the lower half of the mine. Gather soldiers to tighten security higher up."

"Understood!"

"Also, tell the miners to collapse any tunnels halfway up the mountain and lower. We don't want the enemy getting in any of them."

"I'll see to it immediately!"

The messenger rushed out of the tent. The only one left, Ninym turned to Wein.

"Can we hold out?"

"Doubt it." His reply was concise. "We've kept control of the situation by restricting their attack routes to the mountain paths. If they carve out their own way of climbing up, it'll become a battle of attrition. Once that happens, we haven't got a chance."

"You mean, we wouldn't have a chance if nothing changes. Right?"

"Exactly." He smiled. "I'll leave Hagal to command here. Step back and support him, Ninym."

"Okay—but don't die, Wein."

"How could I? I'm leaving my heart here. I don't see why I would," he cooed, stroking her hair lightly. And with that, he left the tent.

Waiting outside for him was Raklum.

"Your Highness."

"Raklum, how are we looking?"

"Everything is ready. We can depart at any time."

Wein nodded in satisfaction. "Time to pay his dumb mug a visit."

At the gold mine, the battle raged on, mostly one-sided.

The Marden forces bypassed the mountain roads by stretching long ladders up the cliffs to climb them one by one, like ants swarming a giant mountain of sugar.

Despite their superior skills, the Natra soldiers were clearly outnumbered. They'd fortified the upper half of the mountain and did their best to keep the enemy back, but even from the foot of the gold mine, it was evident they were slowly being picked off.

"General, our units are overpowering them in all directions!" reported an animated voice, a messenger.

Anyone could tell the tides had shifted in Marden's favor at long last.

"Then it's only a matter of time before they surrender," said one of Draghwood's commanders.

Around the room, the officers in the headquarters wore bright, optimistic expressions. But then Draghwood addressed them sternly.

"Don't grow careless. You don't know what desperate acts a savage will do when cornered," he growled. "Is the back of the mine under control?"

"Yes. Even if the enemy tries to escape, we have enough men in position to stop them. Sir Logan has taken command, so there should be no issues."

"Good. If they do spy any of those beasts, show no mercy. We'll make sure every single one rots on this land," he spat.

Just as Draghwood was gloating in his grandstanding, he could see a few Marden cavalrymen rush into their tent.

"The general! Where is General Draghwood?! There's an urgent message from Captain Logan!"

The voice traveled far for all to hear. The commanders looked at one another, anxious to hear the news. Any urgent news had never been good for them. Did something happen at the back end of the hill?

"…I'll hear it. Get the messengers."

"S-sir! Hey, you guys over there! The general is this way!"

Called over by the commanders, the messengers dismounted their horses and ran to Draghwood and knelt in front of him.

"Report. What did Logan say?"

"Yes. Um…," a messenger said falteringly, placing down a knapsack and flinging it open to reveal its contents.

Logan's head rolled in front of Draghwood.

Huh—? Everyone's mind went blank for a few seconds.

The messenger stomped on the ground to fill the silence and unsheathed his sword in one fluid movement. "—He said he'd meet you on the other side."

With a sharp flash of light, the blade sliced through Draghwood, and he collapsed backward into a heap, his eyes frozen wide in shock. As his armor hit the ground and made a piercing shrill, time finally began to move again.

"B-bastards, what are you— Gah?!"

The commanders had all drawn their weapons, but the messengers were faster, carving their swords through the gathered men and cutting them down. With that, spears rained down from outside the tent and dispatched the rest of the officers in the blink of an eye.

"Your Highness, it's done."

"Good work," the man who'd struck Draghwood answered simply. He looked at the fallen general. "…Huh, you're still alive?"

Fresh blood seeped out of the crevices in his shredded armor onto the ground, but Draghwood drew a ragged breath as he glared at his attacker.

"I knew it—I'm no good with swords," the messenger said.

"Guh… *Koff!* Bastard, you're…"

"What, do I remind you of someone?" he asked as he took off his helmet.

He was a young boy with facial features one might dare to call cherubic. It was a face Draghwood knew.

"You… You're Wein…!" he gasped.

"It's our first time meeting face-to-face like this, isn't it, General Draghwood?" Tossing aside his helmet, Wein Salema Arbalest gave a wide smile.

"Why? Why are you here…?!"

"Well, I came to take your head. You've been a bad boy, Draghwood. All this fighting left your headquarters wide-open.

"Gngh…!"

As Draghwood glared up at him with malice, he noticed the sword lying beside Wein's feet. His wounds burned, scorching hot against his skin. The taste of iron filled his mouth. He just needed to grab the sword. If he could buy time, someone would realize there was a problem at the headquarters.

"No one's coming," Wein said.

Bull's-eye. Draghwood's shoulders trembled.

"My soldiers are stationed all around this tent, and every last one of yours is busy on the mountain. Short of a fire breaking out, they won't give this place a second thought."

"You talk like you know everything…!"

"I *do* know everything. It's how I got this far."

"What?!"

Wein shrugged his shoulders indifferently at the dying Draghwood, who was desperately refusing to back down.

"I wanted to see if we could keep the Marden army at bay by getting them caught up in the frenzied fighting on the battlefield. That was my basic plan. It funny, isn't it? It's a lot harder to exhibit restraint when you're at an advantage. Your army—from soldiers on the outskirts to you guys here at the center—were restless today. We've been up there watching you scramble around for three weeks, you know. Finding a way to slip in was way too easy."

"……" Draghwood opened his mouth to object, but his current situation was proof enough.

He was mortified, but he tried his best to dig through his mind for clues to how this could have happened—and came to a sudden realization. "Wait! I knew a small army of yours was coming down the mountain! I even received reports on who was in command."

"Impossible. After all, we never came down the mountain."

Draghwood's eyes swam. *How the hell did they get here if they didn't come down the mountain?*

"You remember the tunnel in the cave, right?"

His consciousness was fading away. "N-no way, they said clearing the debris from the cave-in would take months…"

"Next to that." Wein smiled merrily. "The miners dug us a tunnel right next to it beforehand: one leading right from the mine to the cave."

"——" His entire body shook. "Im…possible."

"The purpose of the cave-in wasn't to get rid of Marden soldiers. It was to make you forget about the cave altogether."

Everything Draghwood had mounted and piled together, all his awards and achievements as a proud military man, came crashing down upon him. Whether he liked it or not, Draghwood knew this boy outmatched him as a leader in every way.

"Then, all we had to do was open up a new tunnel, put on your armor, and go outside. No one would ever guess we were Natra men. We just happened to run into Logan on the way here."

"…So you're saying we were wrapped around your finger this entire time?" Draghwood coughed out.

Look. The sword. By his foot. You can still move. Accept it. You failed as a leader. But you can still have his head.

"Heh… Heh-heh, *koff*, bwa-ha-ha-ha-ha." Draghwood laughed as he continued to gush blood. Laughed and laughed and laughed, then— "HAAAAAAAAAAAAAH!"

Collecting the last of his strength, he dived with all his might for the sword by Wein's foot.

"Well, this wasn't really part of the official plan, but—" Wein plunged his sword through the general's torso as it writhed on the ground. "I swore I'd cut down any who insult my heart."

A single gleam. And his body split in two, slumping onto the floor.

"Later, Draghwood." Wein wiped the blood off his blade and sheathed it in the scabbard.

Beside him, Raklum had removed his helmet to bow reverently.

"That was marvelous, Your Highness."

"You call this 'marvelous'? …Oh, c'mon, why are you crying, Raklum?"

"My apologies. I was so moved by your swordsmanship…"

"…Okay, okay. We better get going. I might have said otherwise, but their troops at the back of the mine might send people over once they realize Logan's gone."

"We'll continue to set their base ablaze according to your plan, correct?"

"Right. Focus mainly on food and supplies. We've got to make it clear something's wrong and throw them in a panic so the rest of our men can crush them. Let's go."

"Understood!"

They hopped back on their horses and lowered their torches to engulf the camp in flames. It spread in an instant, and the corpses of Draghwood and his men were swallowed up in the dancing fire. The ash quickly rose into the sky, sending a message to the soldiers fighting on the upper levels of the mine.

"H-hey, look over there!" "Is that fire coming from the headquarters?" "Wait! Is this another attack by the enemy?"

No Marden soldier had forgotten the fire from the nighttime raid. They carried the trauma of those flames, and for this reason, their composures began to crumble as chaos spread among them. When the messengers reported the deaths of Draghwood and the other commanders, their hesitation grew fatal.

There were those who resisted, those who tried to withdraw, and those who were simply dumfounded. Without any guidance, the Marden soldiers had lost the power to fight. As the number of casualties grew, the Marden forces practically tumbled down to the foot of the mountain in retreat.

The sun was beginning to set as Wein and the others made it back up to the summit. They were greeted with praises and cheers from the soldiers, whose blood was still boiling from the heat of battle.

"Oh! His Highness has returned!"

"Your Highness, I'm glad to see you in good health!"

"The strategy worked like a charm!"

Most of the soldiers were injured. The death toll wasn't that small, either. But their faces were lively and energetic as they celebrated Wein's safe return and extolled his praises.

"You did extraordinarily well, every last one of you! There is no doubt today that we delivered a heavy blow against the Marden! Victory is close at hand! Think of this as our final hurrah and stay focused!"

"YEAAAAAAAAAH!" The soldiers' war cry shook the earth.

Wein moved forward to walk among them and share a quick word or two with each one. The old general Hagal was waiting for him in the distance.

"Hagal, thanks for holding down the fort while I was gone."

"No such thanks are needed." He bowed reverently.

"I'd like to hear an update on the current situation. What's going on with Marden?"

"Of course. They've given up on sieging the mine. I believe they're now strengthening their defenses on more level ground some distance away. From their current location, I'm guessing there's no possibility of another attack."

"Probably because they're fighting over who'll succeed as leader and whether to continue the war."

"Do you believe they will, Your Highness?"

"Not a chance," he said with conviction. "We've proved to Marden that they were overexcited for a war that turned into a huge failure. That must have killed any remaining morale. Not to mention most of them were burned to a crisp. I bet the commanders will put all the blame on the late Draghwood and decide to withdraw. Well, if anyone takes command here and fails, they'll have to take on the responsibility for losing this war."

"That makes sense," Hagal agreed with a nod.

Then comes a meeting to reach an agreement and reconcile… That's my real battle.

Wein couldn't fail this time. He'd palm off this dud of a mine back to Marden using every last trick he had.

I need to start laying the groundwork. I'll have Ninym help out, too…

With that in mind, Wein came to a sudden realization.

"By the way, where's Ninym?"

"Lady Ninym is going around to each group, checking on their injuries and casualties. She should return shortly."

"I see. Well, let's have a little pre-victory drink until she gets back."

Just as he was about to ask Hagal to join him, an uproar came from the edge of the mine. They looked at each other and immediately ran toward the source.

"What's wrong? What happened?"

"Ah, Y-Your Highness, well... Please look over there." The soldier on guard pointed at the plains the Marden were occupying.

Wein looked over and could hardly believe his eyes.

The Marden army was marching farther and farther away.

"Does this mean...they're withdrawing?"

With their backs to Natra as they slouched toward the border, the army was clearly withdrawing. There was no other explanation.

But Wein had his reservations. Sure, it'd be great if they pulled out completely, but it was happening way too soon. Anyone with the power and rank to make this decision should have already joined Draghwood in the afterworld.

"Hagal, do you think they're trying to fake us out?"

"...No, from the looks of it, it seems like they are retreating. In their current state, the soldiers wouldn't be willing to pull such a petty trick."

"......"

Nnnghhh. Wein groaned inside.

It's not that he *wasn't* happy about Marden retreating so quickly. The sooner they left, the sooner they could start negotiating. But he still couldn't help but think something else was going on.

"Um, Your Highness, pardon me, but..." A timid soldier next to them suddenly spoke up. "Could it be this really means we won...?"

Wein noticed the thousands of soldiers around him shifting their gaze from him to the retreating army, back and forth.

What should he tell them? Wein considered for a moment.

"Everyone, listen up! The Marden have turned their backs on us and are running home!"

Even the farthest soldiers turned their ears to listen to his announcement.

"However, it very well may be the start of a despicable plan against us! All the same, if they're using an underhanded tactic, they have all but admitted they're no match for us!" he thundered. "Therefore, I shall make a declaration right here! —We Natra have won this war!"

The area around the gold mine was hushed. There wasn't a single peep.

Then, in the next moment, cheers erupted from the soldiers with the same force as a bomb explosion.

"Let me hear your triumphant cries! Let the Marden know we are the victors!" Wein encouraged.

They gave a resounding hoot that flooded the surrounding area and was loud enough to shake bones.

"Is this all right?" Hagal whispered into his ear.

Wein nodded. "There's no doubt they're up to something and will be ready to strike back soon enough. We're preparing by boosting morale. Don't drop your guard, Hagal."

"As you wish." He bowed respectfully.

Weaving her way through the hooting crowd, Ninym appeared before the two. "So this is where you were, Your Highness."

"Oh, Ninym… What's wrong?" Wein could sense something was off. "I heard you'd been examining the injured. Is it worse than we thought?"

"No, our soldiers actually suffered less than expected." She shook her head. "It's something else. Your Highness, we just received word from one of our spies in the royal capital of Marden."

"Oh? What? Did Fyshtarre get so mad he went on a vassal-killing spree?"

"They've surrendered," she reported.

"........." It took Wein several seconds to process this information. "Surrendered?"

"Yes."

"Marden?"

"Yes."

"...To whom and how?"

"To the neighboring country of Kavalinu. They were unable to hold out against the large-scale assault, since the majority of their troops were fighting here, and...King Fyshtarre was killed, so..."

What the hell was Marden doing? How the hell could Fyshtarre be so friggin' dumb?

As various curses tore through the back of Wein's mind, the more present half of his consciousness was able to arrive at a more important issue.

"Hey, Ninym... We were supposed to meet with Marden after this, right? To reach an agreement?" Wein somehow managed to speak with a bit of civility. "What do you think will happen if we try now...?"

Ninym couldn't meet his eyes and answered apprehensively. "Seeing they've been destroyed, I imagine it'd fall through..."

"......"

Huh. So that's it.

It'd just fall through.

Wein gave a small sigh and looked up at the sky.

Then he screamed.

"WHAT. THE. HEEEEEEELLLLLL?!"

His futile cries were swallowed up by the soldiers' happy chants and faded away.

The Kingdom of Natra was on the northernmost point of the continent, where summers were short. Just as the sun's rays grew strong and the vegetation verdant, fall and winter would come knocking on its door. Such was its weather.

But it also meant its townspeople knew how to enjoy summer to its fullest. Visitors to this land would often find people jovially going about their day. Festivals and laughter in the Kingdom of Natra usually continued late into the night around this time of year.

But unlike the merriment in the nearby castle town, Wein was splayed across the desk in his office, wallowing in self-pity.

"How did this happen...?"

It'd been one month since the end of the war with Marden over the Jilaat gold mine. Hagal had stayed behind to guard it, while Wein returned home to deal with the massive pileup of government affairs and continued to gather intel on Marden.

The entire continent soon heard the news of Marden's fall to Kavalinu. It may have been a small northern country, but it was a country nonetheless. The collapse of a nation and the end of its history would interest anyone involved in politics. Especially because Marden had a gold mine. It was common knowledge that Marden and Natra fought over it, but everyone wanted to know how this land would be dealt with in the end.

The Kingdom of Natra pretty much stole it from under their noses.

The Kingdom of Marden wouldn't stand for it and fought back.

The Kingdom of Kavalinu destroyed Marden in the meantime.

Considering this series of events, the mine would normally be considered Natra's territory now—but the caveat was whether Kavalinu would allow that.

And sure enough, this was the day Natra and Kavalinu had planned to meet and hopefully come to an agreement.

"—Excuse me." The office door opened, and Ninym walked in. The moment she saw Wein lying across the desk, she gave a look that said *Oh*. "Your meeting with the messenger from Kavalinu didn't work out?"

"...Nope," he mournfully croaked, looking up at the ceiling theatrically. "I COULDN'T GET RID OF THE MIIIIINE! SHIIIIIT!"

His plan to sell the dried-up mine back to Marden for a high price woefully fell apart after Kavalinu destroyed them.

But Wein hadn't given up hope yet. Kavalinu desperately wanted the mine. Or rather, they weren't above invasion to get what they wanted. Their plan had likely been to engage the battle-weary Marden once Natra had been defeated and then take both the country and its gold mine in one go.

Meaning Kavalinu had been thrown a curveball, too. They wanted the mine *now*, even if they had to take it by force. But they needed to think twice before dipping their toes in an unanticipated war. And so, Wein looked for any possible advantages and quickly sent messengers to Kavalinu to set up a meeting so he could pawn the mine off on them.

But this dream was not realized.

"Wasn't there talk about the Marden royal family escaping from Kavalinu's hands?"

"Yes, according to the information in our spy reports. We've heard the royal family is rallying the defeated troops that returned from the battle for the mine, lying low, and forming a resistance movement against Kavalinu."

"It seems like they're having a pretty hard time keeping their grip on Marden. A two-front war with us would spell bad news, so they did their best to push a nonaggression pact. They insisted we keep the mine in exchange, so I had no momentum."

"Oh dear."

Kavalinu was a Western nation, so Ninym wasn't present for their meeting, but she imagined Wein's bitter expression—as if he'd ground his teeth on a mouthful of insects—and giggled.

"Hey, hey, this is no laughing matter, Ninym. Read this report. The costs of all the people, material, and money for this war! Thanks to that, the national treasury is empty! There's nothing left! And our prize? Some dried-up old mine! AGHHHHHHHH, COOOOOOOME OOOOOOOON!"

As Wein held his head and writhed in agony, Ninym walked over and thrust a bunch of papers under his nose. "Well then, here. A little present for you."

"What's this? Love letters from the ladies? I mean, I *am* a supercool guy for beating an army of thirty thousand, right?"

"I would have torn up and thrown those away. It's a report from Pelynt."

The miners who'd participated in the fight were rewarded medals of honor. Pelynt, who had acted as mediator, now worked as a mine inspector for them.

"Okay, so it's a report. No big deal… Huh?" Wein quickly flipped through the report, and his eyes stopped. "More gold…has been discovered… Wait, seriously?"

"I personally went over there to investigate, and it's true. I wouldn't call it another gold rush, but it could mean we'll turn a profit."

"Ohhhhh…" He sighed deeply, leaning against the back of his chair. "I've been trying to plan a good time to tell my troops that the mine is a bust, but I guess there's still a shred of hope left."

"With your reputation now, I think you'll be fine even without the mine. The people adore you, you're proven in battle, and your political savviness is second to none. Many believe you'll be the wisest, most benevolent ruler to date."

"Nah, approval ratings are temporary. My failures will be what sticks forever. Carelessness is our greatest enemy, Ninym," he warned.

She gave a wry smile and sighed at his obstinance. He could master-fully craft all the daring schemes he wanted on the battlefield, but he always returned to his normal self at the palace. Even so, his methods had helped solve a number of national crises, so she supposed there wasn't too much of an issue.

"But, wow, who knew? Turns out we might be able to use the mine after all. I guess that gives me a little elbow room. I've been so busy since I got back. I might even take a few naps around here."

"No." She placed a pen on the mountain of papers in front of Wein.

"...After I finish this, then?"

"Nope, there's more."

"......"

"Ambassadors of several nations have requested to meet with you. The civil officials would like to discuss the budget. There's also the pressing issue of supplying the military with new arms and equipment. Oh, and Her Highness Princess Falanya misses you. You've delayed inspecting a town for the war as well. The list goes on and on."

A meticulously itemized, overbooked schedule. Even though he'd overcome a national crisis, new challenges were already cropping up one after the other. Wein gave a small sigh and yelled.

"LET'S JUST SELL THIS COUNTRY OFF AND GET THE HELL OUTTA HEEEEEEERE!"

Wein earnestly howled in agony, but alas that, too, dissolved into nothing.

The death of the Emperor of Earthworld set off a disturbing series of events across the continent. In time, the curtain would rise on an age known as the Great War of Kings.

Afterword

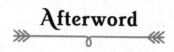

Hello, it's nice to meet you. To some of you, long time no see. This is Toru Toba. Thank you for picking up *The Genius Prince's Guide to Raising a Nation Out of Debt: Hey, How About Treason?*

How did you like this book?

Its topic is what you might call "governance."

Governance: It's seen as a vague, difficult, troubling topic. The more you look into it, the tougher this undertaking seems.

But at the same time, a nation isn't something that moves by way of some invisible force working outside the bounds of mortal knowledge. It's run entirely by human hands.

And because it's run by humans, there are countless times when people have come together, racking their brains to decide on a solution, only for it to fail. Or just when they expect success, foreign countries might interfere or natural phenomena could cause some chaos, making them stumble in unpredictable directions. Other times, they might succeed without any major obstacles, winding up in a situation where they ought to give themselves a round of applause.

I think everyone has more or less oscillated between this kind of joy and sorrow.

Governance is about human behavior—a complex, tangled thing involving the thoughts and feelings of all kinds of people.

In this book, I wanted to put a spotlight on the main character's mood swings. I'm sure there are readers who will glance through this section before reading the main text, so I can't go into too much detail here, but I'd feel blessed as the author if you grow to love this hardworking hero burdened with the important task of running a government.

To switch subjects, I've been going on a lot of small outings lately. I used to be an extreme homebody, but one day, I started thinking I really couldn't keep living that way. I've been doing different kinds of day trips to popular tourist destinations.

I mostly visit shrines and temples. But I've noticed how convenient public transportation is as I go back and forth to these spots. Spend a few hours swaying on a train, and you can get pretty much wherever you need to. When you stop and think about it, that's pretty incredible.

We're always trying to shorten travel time. I wonder how far our innovations will go. I've recently heard of developments in personal aircraft. It seems as if the possibility of flying though the sky alone might be possible within my own lifetime...or maybe not... But I would've never imagined smartphones and tablets as a child, and now they're a part of everyday life. So perhaps it's not out of the realm of possibility? Just as we speak of the steam engine trains with nostalgia, one day we'll probably talk about the train like that, too...probably.

Personally, I find that these developments are fun and exciting, but they also make me question my own standards and common sense as a kid... I'm going to try not to be left behind by these new technological advancements. Then again, I still don't even have a smartphone.

Well, this is where I give my thanks and advertise.

First of all, a big thanks to Ohara for helping me out with this book. Thank you for being there to guide me from the planning stages to the final plot and text. Because of you, I could give the readers a polished story. I look forward to working with you in the future.

And to my illustrator, fal_maro, thank you for your beautiful illustrations. As the author, I'm always excited to see my work come to life, and I wholeheartedly approved each one of your illustrations as my editor sent them to me. Especially the third color insert. Yes, it was very nice.

Thank you to all my fellow authors for their valuable insights. I'm especially grateful to Akamitsu Awamura for the detailed advice.

By the way, it looks like GA Bunko will publish Awamura's new work *100 Years War of 100 Gods* in June. It's a battle fantasy where gods fight one another for imperial dominance, and just by the synopsis, I can already tell it'll show you a whole new world. Be sure to check it out!

And last but not least, to all the readers, thank you for putting this book in your hands. With an overwhelming number of books published each month, it must seem like an unending flood of books to you, but I'm truly honored you chose mine out of so many.

From now on, I will do my best to create more interesting books. Please look forward to it. Well then, let's meet in the next one.

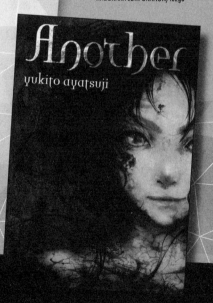